Praise for Michael Baron's
National Bestseller Leaves:

"Beautifully written, memorable and realistic, you will not want the book to end once you start it. Everyone will be anxiously awaiting the next book. Do not miss *Leaves* by Michael Baron."
– Single Titles

"This wonderful blend of irony, love and humor is one of my favorite books this year."
– Cheryl's Book Nook

"Baron has the gift and ability to sweep you away from reality into the story like the winds of autumn sweeps the last leaves off the trees. The characters are so lifelike that they become one's own family."
– CMash Reads

"*Leaves* is plainly a lovely, lovely story that will be enjoyed by all readers. Sometimes, potency is conveyed without a stick of dynamite because it is just so – like most of our lives – very real! Grand job, Michael Baron!"
– Crystal Book Reviews

"The charm of Michael Baron's writing brings a special polish to a poignant story, making it sparkle and enchant like October leaves in N̶ England."
– Long and Short Rev.

T0163144

Everything
or
Nothing

Everything
or
Nothing

Michael
Baron

THE
STORY PLANT

Also by Michael Baron:

When You Went Away
Crossing the Bridge
The Journey Home
Spinning
Anything
A Winter Discovery

<u>The Gold Family Stories</u>
Leaves
Recovery
An Anniversary Feast

This is a work of fiction. Names, characters, places, and in-cidents either are the product of the author's imagination or are used fictitiously. Any resemblance to actual events, locales, organizations, or persons living or dead, is entirely coincidental and beyond the intent of either the author or the publisher.

The Story Plant
Studio Digital CT, LLC
P.O. Box 4331
Stamford, CT 06907

Copyright © 2014 by The Fiction Studio
Cover design by Barbara Aronica-Buck

Print ISBN-13: 978-1-61188-147-9
E-book ISBN-13: 978-1-61188-148-6

Visit our website at www.TheStoryPlant.com and the au-thor's website at www.MichaelBaronBooks.com

All rights reserved, which includes the right to reproduce this book or portions thereof in any form whatsoever, except as provided by US Copyright Law. For information, address The Story Plant.

First Story Plant Printing: September 2014

Printed in The United States of America
0 9 8 7 6 5 4 3 2 1

Chapter 1

Soon after his son Joey started walking, Maxwell Gold nicknamed the boy "Pinball" after his pronounced knack for bouncing off of things. Anything, really — walls, furniture, people. The boy was likely to smack against even the most inconsequential bit of matter — a random quark floating through space, if such a thing were possible. Joey went from his first steps to full-tilt running in the space of a week. Caution had been considerably slower to develop; it was only partially developed now that he'd reached the age of three.

At this very moment, Joey wasn't a pinball. He was a bowling ball — with Maxwell playing the role of the pin. Joey backed across the living room until his butt came up against the couch. He then ran toward his father, who was sitting on the floor. On contact, Maxwell crashed backward, grabbing Joey as he did this so they both wound up splayed on the ground as though they'd been thrown from an exploding building. Maxwell would then make an elaborate show, to his child's delight, of pulling himself back up. *Whoa, that was a big one, Joe. I'm not sure how much more of this my body can take!*

This was the fourteenth time they'd done this over the course of the past half-hour. It might even have been the fifteenth or sixteenth; Maxwell was beginning to lose count. Joey thought it was hilarious every single time. And if Joey thought it was funny, then Maxwell would continue to play his part as long as his son wanted. If the past was any indication, Joey could just as easily glance over at the toy chest while he was backing up this time, see the Nerf football, and decide that he wanted to have a catch instead. He might even eye the television and decide that it was time for some cartoons.

It didn't play out that way, though. For the fifteenth/sixteenth/seventeenth time, Joey came barreling toward Maxwell, and Maxwell surprised himself by catching him, rolling, and doing a complete flip before they stretched out on the floor. This seemed to bewilder Joey nearly as much as it did Maxwell himself, and they shared an expression of disbelief for a second before erupting in laughter.

They were still laughing when Annie came into the living room. "You're not breaking anything, are you?" she said in her mom voice.

Maxwell looked in Annie's direction and chuckled. "I think I might have sprained my ACL on that last one, but all of the furniture is intact."

"That's good to hear. We don't want another coffee table incident." Annie arched her eyebrows in mock recrimination. At least Maxwell thought it was "mock." A couple of years ago, he would have known for sure.

Annie half-turned away from them. "I'm heading out."

Maxwell tried to remember if they'd discussed morning plans earlier. "Oh, okay. I was thinking we'd all go to lunch later. Joey was saying something about tacos earlier, though it's possible he was saying he wanted some to smash into the carpet."

Annie took a quick glimpse at her son, who was still lying on the floor with his arms outstretched after his last act of demolition. Her lips turned upward slightly.

"I'm not sure I'll be back by lunch."

Had they talked about plans? Maxwell knew that Annie hated it when he forgot what she was doing, but he had absolutely no memory of any conversation about today.

"Um, okay. When do you think you will be back?"

Her eyes narrowed. That could mean she was peeved that he'd forgotten their discussion about her plans, or it could mean that she didn't like being questioned. Maxwell could read Annie just about as well as he could read the translation of one of his favorite books into a language he didn't know.

"I'm really not sure," she said. "I'll text you if it's getting too late."

With that, she knelt down to Joey, kissed him on the forehead, and left.

Six months ago, Maxwell might have been surprised that she didn't kiss him as well. Now, he just watched her go and allowed a few seconds for the mood to resettle in the room. Then, from his place on the ground, he turned to his son, who was still lying flat.

"Ready?"

Joey seemed a bit lost for a moment, then smiled, stood up, and faced his father, beginning to back up as he had on the previous however-many occasions. Once again, he steamed ahead. As Joey ran toward him, Maxwell tried to think of another way to change things up. There were only so many times something like this could remain funny, right? Even a three-year-old would find this monotonous if Maxwell didn't go in a different direction, no?

As Joey hit, Maxwell didn't tumble over. Instead, he exclaimed, "Boing!" and shook as though Joey had rattled him to the core. He figured that doing the unexpected would make Joey laugh even harder.

Instead, Joey sat on the floor, his face crumpled, and he started to cry.

Maxwell wasn't completely unprepared for this. There had been a few times in the past months when Joey's mood would change instantaneously, pivoting from joy to misery in a moment. Still, Maxwell always found it upsetting; increasingly so, actually. At this point, tears were streaming down Joey's face and the boy was pounding the carpet with one fist.

As he did after each occurrence, Maxwell gathered Joey up, moved to the couch, and held him close while he cried. If this instance was like the others – and it wasn't always crying; sometimes it was squealing, other times throwing things, and once holding his breath – the episode would go on for five minutes or so, followed by another twenty minutes of quiet where neither of them were allowed to move. Maxwell had come to learn that there was nothing to be gained from trying to talk Joey through it or employing any other parenting tool. The cycle had to run its course.

So Maxwell pulled Joey close to him and they sat, Maxwell trying with decreasing effectiveness to convince himself that this was simply a phase.

On Monday, the campaign was back on. Up to this point, Maxwell had been able to focus most of his efforts at becoming Oldham's next mayor to weekdays, keeping weekends for his family and himself (to the degree he did anything exclusively for himself these days). It was August now, though, and he knew it wouldn't be possible to maintain this schedule. He was going to need to get out in front of people more often and, considering how much of Oldham's voting population worked outside of the town, that meant getting in front of them when they were around during evenings, weekends, and even early morning meet-and-greets at the train station. He was, in fact, scheduled to speak at an arts-and-music festival next Saturday, and there were several other items like this on the calendar in the coming weeks.

"I just don't think anyone is going to want to hear me talk about single-stream recycling at this event," he said to Steve Jordan, one of the young strategists Mike Mills had brought onto the team when Mike agreed to serve as campaign manager. Steve's strength was data. He could slice and dice information in ways that illuminated the dark corners of voter inclination. This was hugely valuable, but Steve still wanted to be seen as something other than an analyst; he really wanted to be known as a Big Idea guy.

Steve tapped on the iPad that was as much a physical feature as his nose. "It's an issue that can generate some heat here and it's an area of clear distinction between you and Mayor Bruce."

Maxwell was about to reiterate his disagreement when Mike stepped in.

"Maxwell is right on this one, Steve," Mike said. "We'll have plenty of time to get to this, especially during the debates. It's going to be a beautiful summer afternoon and people will be going to the festival just to enjoy themselves. They don't want to think about garbage."

Steve shook his head. "We shouldn't be missing any opportunities at this point."

Mike held up his hand. "The right opportunity needs to come in the right venue. Let's go with the upgrade in music education that has scored some points for us in the past. People will have their kids with them and they're going to be listening to good music. Maxwell can hit hard on how the mayor has allowed school arts budgets to be slashed repeatedly and suggest indirectly that, if they want to keep enjoying events like this one, they'd better vote a new man into office."

"Yes, I'm much more comfortable with that," Maxwell said. "This is where we can start to get across our differences on education. Those are very real."

Steve didn't seem convinced, but Maxwell knew that it didn't matter. At twenty-three, Steve hadn't learned when to cut his losses — Maxwell was sure the subject of single-stream recycling would come up at least three more times this afternoon — but he was enough of a team player to work aggressively on the agenda, even when it wasn't his agenda.

For the next half-hour, the three of them hammered out the talking points of the speech Maxwell would deliver. Being a product of the Oldham public school system and having watched his niece and nephew educated in some of the same schools, Maxwell knew that all programs outside of the core curricula were being de-funded aggressively. It was an issue all over the state of Connecticut, but the numbers showed that the conditions in Oldham were worse than most. If Mayor Bruce continued to hold office and have strong influence over the Board of Education, there was a good chance that Joey wouldn't even pick up a paintbrush in elementary school.

Mike stood from the conference room table, which caused Maxwell to realize that he hadn't even shifted in his seat since this planning session had started.

"I'm going to get some coffee." Mike said. "Can I get either of you anything?"

Maxwell was about to ask Mike to bring him a cup when Cynthia Robinson, one of the aides volunteering for the campaign, entered the room.

"I have the results of the phone poll," she said, holding up a piece of paper.

Mike moved quickly to take the paper from Cynthia. Maxwell sat up in his chair, the coffee suddenly unnecessary. Mike studied the numbers wordlessly for what seemed like an hour before making eye contact with Maxwell and offering a little shrug.

"They're that bad?" Maxwell said.

Steve rose to get a view of the numbers and Mike glanced back down at the paper before looking up again at Maxwell. "The education message has some resonance, as does the issue of expanded commercial development."

Maxwell tilted his head. "The last phone poll said the same thing. What's different this time?"

"Bruce is scoring far bigger points on the budget than we anticipated."

Maxwell groaned. "Bruce uses part of the budget to pay for renovations on his house. Voters like that?"

Steve moved back to the table. "We aren't driving home the corruption angle. Maybe you need to get him a little bloody there."

Maxwell wasn't convinced that the problem was that voters were unaware of Bruce's ties to illegal activities. Maxwell's candidacy was born from a scandal involving the mayor last fall — a scandal that Mike's newspaper trumpeted on the front page for much longer than the traditional news cycle. No, people knew that Bruce was shady and had been for as long as he'd been involved with Oldham politics. Maybe they just didn't care.

"What's the bottom line?" Maxwell said.

Mike studied the paper again, which Maxwell knew was purely a delay tactic. Maxwell was sure that the very first thing Mike looked at when he got the document was how respondents were likely to vote.

"Bruce is up by twelve points."

Maxwell fell back in his chair.

Mike sat down again and put the poll results between them. "It's August. People are still getting to know you."

Maxwell scoffed. "I've lived in Oldham most of my life and I've hardly been low-profile. I seriously doubt name recognition is an issue."

Mike gestured to acknowledge that Maxwell had a valid point. "Still, it's early.

You have plenty of time to make up twelve points."

Steve leaned forward. "You could make up a few of those points this weekend if you talked about single-stream recycling."

Maxwell fixed Steve with a glance that suggested he might not want to bring up that topic for another geological era or two. Then he turned back to Mike.

"Yes, I have time to make up twelve points. But are we forgetting that I was down *nine* points last month? I'm not making *up* at this stage; I'm making *down*."

That quieted the room. Nothing more needed to be said. Maxwell didn't need an empty pep talk, and he didn't need to hear that it was possible for underdogs to win. He just needed all of this to sink in. And then he needed to find a way to get his points across more effectively. If he couldn't, November was going to be an awfully cold month, and he was going to be feeling awfully foolish for risking as much as he had to go after this goal.

∿

For whatever reason, it was always tougher getting Joey to bed on Monday nights. Maybe this had something to do with reestablishing his routine after the weekend. Maybe it had to do with the fact that Monday always tended to be a catch-up day at work (especially now with the campaign), which led to rushed dinners and a smaller window between the end of the meal and the point when they sat in Joey's room reading him bedtime stories.

Tonight had been even more of an issue than usual. First, Joey wouldn't brush his teeth, claiming that the toothpaste — the same toothpaste he'd been using for the past year — was "spicy." Maxwell wound up brushing Joey's teeth for him, something he'd never done before and something he was hoping wasn't destined to become a part of their evening ritual. Then Joey insisted on putting his pajama pants over his head. He seemed to think this was hilarious, and Maxwell found it funny the first time the boy did it as well. The fourth time wasn't nearly as humorous, and if it had gotten to an eighth or ninth time, it would have been very difficult to keep the impatience from his face.

Once they'd read a couple of picture books, Annie left as she always did and Maxwell and Joey entered the last phase of the bedtime process. Maxwell climbed into bed next to his son and sang him the lullaby that Maxwell's mother used to sing to Maxwell. It was obvious to Maxwell that Joey already didn't remember his grandmother, who died before Joey's second birthday, but he seemed to like knowing that his dad was singing him to sleep with a song that his mom once used to sing her son to sleep. On most nights, this was enough to get the boy to settle. Tonight, though, as Maxwell kissed his forehead, Joey wrapped his arms around his father's neck.

"One more," the boy said.

"One more what?"

"One more."

Maxwell lay his head back down, which caused Joey to release him and do the same. Did Joey want one more song? One more minute? No elaboration seemed forthcoming, which was typical with Joey's communication at this point. He'd been a little slow to start talking and he didn't seem to be rushing into conversation. Maxwell simply lay there a short while longer and then tried to get up again. As before, Joey latched onto him. The third time this happened, Maxwell decided to sing the song again, this time brushing Joey's hair as he did so. That seemed to make a difference. By the time Maxwell climbed out of the bed, Joey was asleep and Maxwell felt as though he'd put in another full day of work. Maxwell knew that it would be a terrible idea for the kid to grow accustomed to his father staying in bed with him until he nodded off, but that seemed to be the only available option tonight since any move Maxwell made to leave the room activated Joey's barnacle-like qualities.

The odds were good that Joey would sleep through the night now, though. He wasn't always easy to get to bed, but he usually slept heavily once he was down. Given how much energy the boy expended during the day, that seemed like an essential thing.

This meant that the rest of the night was for the grownups, something Maxwell had been looking forward to. Between one thing and another, he'd had very little time alone with Annie recently, and he felt that they needed to take advantage of any chance they might get.

The last nine months had been a series of fits and starts in Maxwell and Annie's marriage, all beginning around the time he decided to run for mayor. Annie didn't want to be stuck at home with Joey while Maxwell was running Oldham, and her response to this peaked right after last year's Halloween party when she took off on her own for three days. Maxwell had never been able to get her to tell him where she'd gone or why she felt the need to leave, but she seemed to come back with a resolve toward bridging the gulf that had opened between them. There continued to be times when she vanished — more often emotionally than physically — but she always came back and there were always stretches afterward where things seemed more like they had once been.

It was a form of progress, one that was somewhat better than the "progress" he was making on the mayoral campaign. Most significantly, though, the inconsistent nature of his relationship with Annie underscored for Maxwell how much he wanted again the prevailing, loving connection they'd had before Joey was born. For most of the past year, he'd had to face the prospect of having less of his wife and consider the possibility of having none of her, and he found the idea of this physically painful. It wasn't that he didn't want to contend with the ramifications of a failed marriage. If things crashed, he knew with absolute certainty that he'd do everything he could to help Joey get through it okay. It was that he flat-out didn't want to lose Annie. The thought of never again having what they once had together drove home for him just how much he wanted her. They had meant so much to each other before the unease set in; it had to be possible to get most, if not all, of that back.

He stopped in the kitchen on the way from Joey's bedroom, got a bottle of Pinot Noir from the wine rack, and poured two glasses, bringing them into the den where Annie was sitting reading a book on her tablet. He kissed the top of her head and handed her a glass. Annie seemed lost in the book and didn't look up at him immediately. It was maybe fifteen seconds before she took the proffered glass from him.

"What's this for?"

Maxwell sat next to her. "For surviving a three-year-old force of nature and still having a few hours before we call it a night."

Annie gave Maxwell a faint smile and then took a small sip of the wine before setting the glass on the coffee table.

Maxwell settled back into the couch and reached out to rub Annie's shoulders. "What are you reading?"

"A serial killer novel."

"Really? You don't usually read that kind of stuff."

She flicked a page and spoke without looking up. "I'm broadening my horizons."

Maxwell wondered if reading excessively violent fiction qualified as "broadening." "Is it any good?"

"Fantastic, actually. I've already downloaded the author's next three books."

Maxwell wasn't sure what to think of this. He continued to rub one of her shoulders with his right hand while he sipped the wine with his left. "What a crazy day. And then Joey had *something* going on in his head. Even more of a challenge than most Mondays." He took a deep breath and exhaled slowly. "Equilibri-um is restored, though."

If Annie had absorbed any of this, she didn't let Maxwell know. Earlier in their mar-riage, Maxwell marveled at Annie's ability to read and maintain a conversation at the same time. That was when she was reading a different kind of fiction, though. Maybe serial killers required all of her attention. He'd just sit here with her until she came up for air.

A few minutes later, Annie sighed, turned off the tablet, and put the device on the cof-fee table. She reached for her wineglass, took another sip, and turned toward him.

"I'm gonna call it a night," she said.

Maxwell glanced at the clock on the cable box. It was 9:37. He started to rise from the couch.

Annie stopped him with a palm. "You don't need to get up. It's early. Relax for a while. I'm just beat."

Maxwell leaned forward. "Are you sure? Maybe an early night would be good for the two of us."

Annie shrugged. "Your call, but I'm wast-ed. I'll probably be out cold before my head hits the pillow."

The message was abundantly clear. It was silly at this point for him to believe that they might have been thinking along the same track. Still, a coincidence would have been welcome.

Maxwell sat back. "Okay. Well, have a good sleep."

Annie started walking toward the bedroom. "Thanks. See you when you come to bed. Well, probably not, actually."

No, probably not, Maxwell thought. He watched his wife head down the hall and then found the television remote and his wineglass. Very little about this evening — or this day, for that matter — had gone according to plan.

Maxwell sat back on his living room couch, feeling decidedly out of his comfort zone.

ᴖᴗ

The next Saturday, Maxwell and Joey were out on their usual "breakfast crawl." The first stop was Rise, a breakfast-only café that had opened in the spring. They served an orange-banana juice that Joey loved and the only granola-yogurt combination he would eat. Maxwell had tried making it for Joey several times, including once after buying both the yogurt and the granola from Rise, and the kid simply wouldn't have it at home or anywhere else.

The wholesome foundation created by this first stage of the morning meal was important, because the next stop on the crawl was The Open Hearth, an Oldham institution since 1970. This stop was all about the coffee cake, something Maxwell had been indulging in for decades. Maxwell had eaten only a fruit salad at Rise because he knew this cake was coming. Owner Carmen Twillie always served him an extra-large square — it seemed that his portions had gotten even larger since he announced his candidacy for mayor — and Maxwell had never once failed to finish the piece, some days even wishing for more. Maxwell didn't worry about Joey stuffing himself here, because Joey still saw the coffee cake as more of a toy than a food; the boy seemed to like the feel of the crumbs as he squeezed them through his fingers and didn't particularly care about getting any in his mouth. Maxwell always felt a little self-conscious about this, thinking that others might be questioning his parenting skills and that Carmen might be considering Joey's destructiveness to be an affront to her hard work, but nearby diners always seemed to chuckle at the sight and Carmen never seemed to be offended. One of the ways in which Maxwell had started to find a special pleasure about having a child was that the kid afforded him multiple opportunities to indulge his inner child. This would sometimes manifest itself in swinging at the playground with Joey on his lap or engaging in physical play, and it very definitely appeared in the form of Carmen's coffee cake. It was so easy to enjoy his piece, because Joey seemed to be having such a great time with his, even if for an entirely different reason.

The final stop on the crawl was the coffee bar 206, which Maxwell had always assumed was named after the area code for Seattle, where America's coffee renaissance began.

He'd subsequently learned that the name was for the water temperature that the owner believed to be ideal for making his brew. Either way, it was Maxwell's favorite place to get coffee on the entirety of Hickory Avenue and he'd limited himself to one cup at The Open Hearth precisely because he wanted a large serving of whatever pour-over Matt Cameron was making today. The fact that Matt served Joey a cup of milk with a shot of decaf espresso — and that Joey loved this — made 206 a necessary stop every Saturday in addition to the several times during the week that Maxwell went there on his way to work. In so many ways, 206 and the other stops on the crawl represented the essence of Oldham — individuals expressing themselves through their mediums for the pleasure of their public. These shops weren't about filling a consumer need; they were about building a constituency from a shared passion. It was the thing Maxwell loved most about his town and the thing he hoped to be able to amplify if the vote went well in November.

They got their drinks and moved to a sidewalk table, settling in like two guys ready to do some serious people-watching.

"There's a green one," Joey said, pointing to a passing car. Last summer, Maxwell had come here with Joey for the first time. They sat outside and, to keep Joey entertained, they identified the colors of the cars as they passed. Since then, Joey did the same thing here and only here.

Joey continued. "There's a red one. There's a yellow one." He paused for a moment. "There's a purple one."

Maxwell hadn't been watching the street as carefully as Joey had been, but the mention of a purple car caught Maxwell's attention. He turned toward where his son was pointing. "That's silver, Joe."

Joey pointed more insistently. "Purple."

Maxwell tilted his head. "We can *pretend* it's purple, if you'd like, but it's really silver."

Joey frowned at him. Maxwell felt chastised. He knew that Joey could distinguish silver from purple; if the boy wanted to play with the names of the colors, why was Maxwell insisting on correcting him? Doing so was hardly going to contribute to his son's development.

"Good morning, Mr. Mayor."

Maxwell turned from the street to the sidewalk. Standing there was Amy Ray. In her late fifties, Amy had lived in Oldham most of her life and had become something of a "kingmaker" in local politics. She was fiercely independent and unwilling to align with a particular party or agenda. Maxwell had known Amy for decades, but had yet to try to court her for his campaign.

"Can I take that as an endorsement?"

Amy smiled politely. "Maxwell, you know I never endorse anyone before October."

"I thought maybe you'd make an exception for an old friend."

Amy's smile seemed warmer now. "Not even for an old friend. How's the campaign going?"

"Great...I think. I don't exactly have a reference point for this. Mike tells me we're doing okay, so I have to believe him."

"Mike's a smart guy."

They both nodded, and then Amy continued. "I'm looking forward to hearing you speak this afternoon. There's supposed to be a great crowd at the festival."

"Well, here's hoping I don't drive them all away."

Amy chuckled. "You'll do fine. So, I haven't seen your wife on the campaign trail yet. Are you keeping her in reserve?"

This wasn't the first time this question had come up, but it was the first time it had come from someone as influential as Amy. Maxwell still hadn't devised the ideal answer for this. He certainly didn't want to say that Annie was ambivalent — at best — about the prospect of his becoming mayor, but he also wasn't willing to promise her presence with him on the stump when he wasn't entirely sure that she'd be making *any* appearances with him even though she'd agreed to a few in the fall.

Maxwell reached out and touched Amy on the arm. "You've met Annie, Amy. You know how charming she is and how easily she wins people over. It didn't seem fair to Mayor Bruce to bring her out so early in the campaign. It wouldn't be sporting."

"So *we are* going to be hearing from your wife?"

This question had come from someone at the next table who Maxwell didn't recognize.

"Gee, I'm starting to think that people might prefer Annie as mayor to me," Maxwell said nervously, pretending he was joking about the nervousness, even though he was getting increasingly uncomfortable.

Maxwell was trying to think of a graceful way to exit this conversation. He even reached into his pocket for his phone, imagining he could use it as a prop to illustrate a pending appointment. At that point, though, Maxwell heard a *splat* on the sidewalk in front of him. He turned toward the sound to find Joey's milk cup leaking onto the street. He got up quickly and looked at his son.

"Joey, what happened?"

It was obvious from the distance between the cup and their table that the boy had thrown the cup, but Maxwell was giving the kid an out. Joey didn't say anything.

Maxwell gave his son a look of recrimination not dissimilar from the one Maxwell had received from Joey earlier. Then he went to pick up the cup. By that point, the contents were everywhere. Joey couldn't have waited to throw it until he'd drunk a little more?

Maxwell used the napkins he had gotten with their order to sop up the mess, supplementing it with napkins offered by the people at the next table. As he was kneeling down to do so, Joey started screaming. These weren't screams of fear or upset, as though Joey was worried about the consequences of his actions. These were screams of defiance.

Without any warning, the kid had gone completely out of control. In front of the patrons of 206.

Potential voters.

Maxwell shunted away that thought quickly, but it had left its mark.

Joey was still screaming when Maxwell stuffed the wet napkins into the milk cup, picked up his own coffee cup, and then lifted his son from the chair upon which he was now standing.

"Sorry," he said to everyone, making brief eye contact with Amy, who was either offering sympathy or disapproval. Then he took his son down the block, back toward their car. By this point, Joey wasn't screaming anymore; now he was just yelling.

Maybe he was going to have to put the breakfast crawl on hold for a while.

~⌣

Every Tuesday for the past two months had included lunch with Mike Mills and potential donors. Maxwell simply wasn't crazy about raising money for himself. He'd orchestrated numerous fundraisers for worthy causes over the years and never had any problem reaching out to everyone he knew to ask for their cash for these purposes. However, he wasn't nearly as aggressive when the money was going into his own pocket (though technically this money wasn't going into his pocket, but into the campaign's coffers; it still felt like the same thing). He never even asked for a raise until his third job. Asking people to donate to his campaign felt a lot like asking his boss for a higher salary, and he just couldn't get comfortable with that. He really wished this was something he could delegate.

Fortunately, Mike had no such compunctions about asking people to open their wallets for Maxwell. On more than one occasion, Maxwell had been walking with Mike on Hickory Avenue and Mike stopped someone he knew, talked about the mayoral campaign, and then asked for a donation right on the spot. This effort, which Maxwell saw as only a few steps above panhandling, always made him cringe inside, but he couldn't argue with its effectiveness. Incongruously, people really were willing to donate if you convinced them it was worth the effort.

The Tuesday lunches were slightly more comfortable for Maxwell. While their guests were always fully aware of the reason for the lunch, it felt less like a hard-sell. They could talk about the community, the issues, their families, and slowly get around to the campaign. And at least they were offering food as well. Today, they'd been lunching with Bill Nelson, owner of Valley Farms, one of Oldham's landmarks and a regional destination. The meal had been going on for nearly an hour, and the conversation had just turned to Maxwell's prospects for taking over the mayor's office.

"Bill, you're going to prosper under any administration," Mike said, "but I think it's inarguable that you'll do even better if everyone in the town is doing better. And more people are going to be doing better with Maxwell as mayor than they ever have under Mayor Bruce."

Bill nodded slowly and turned to Maxwell. "Well, that's why I was looking forward to our getting together. I'd like to hear how

Maxwell is going to improve the lot of the average Oldham citizen."

Maxwell sat forward in his seat. He needed no prompting for this conversation, as he could have rolled out of bed and done fifteen minutes on this topic and really could have for years before he decided to run for office. "It's about using the town's resources to benefit the town, Bill. You know that I've been fighting this battle from my position on the Chamber of Commerce for years. What has become increasingly clear is that Mayor Bruce tends to dole out funds to a narrow few rather than spreading the money around. The town's small business development fund has plenty of money in it, but a tiny group gets to draw on it all the time while a much larger number of very needy business owners have to wade through way more bureaucracy than a place the size of Oldham should ever have."

Bill tipped his head forward. "You're not suggesting that our mayor is corrupt, are you?"

Maxwell wasn't, actually. Still, given the mayor's history, it was nearly guaranteed that Maxwell's lunch mates would bring up corruption at some point. How did Bruce keep getting elected when everyone instantly equated him with illegal acts?

"I think it might be something worse, Bill," Maxwell said. "I think it might be that the mayor is so out of touch with the town's priorities that he doesn't understand where the real need is. He hasn't offered an improvement grant to a single craft shop or gallery in the past three years. And yet the surveys done by the Visitors Center consistently indicate that these shops are one of the primary reasons that visitors come to Oldham."

"Well, I think my farm ranks higher on those surveys."

"Yes, that's true, and with good reason, but those stores on Hickory drive people to spend much more time — and much more money — in town. If they can't make improvements to their storefronts, fewer shoppers are going to want to spend time there. At some point, if too many of these places look tired or wind up closing, people are going to be less enthusiastic about coming to Oldham. That's not good for any of us — even you. There's a pretty big family-friendly farm just a half-hour down the road and there's a town right there that supports *all* of its businesses. If Oldham seems rickety in comparison, some percentage of consumers are going to go there instead of coming all the way here just to go to Valley Farms."

Bill arched his brows. "I think my business is probably okay, Maxwell."

"And I'm sure it is, though very few businesses would anticipate this kind of erosion when things are going well for them. But even if you dismiss that as a threat to Valley Farms' future, you aren't going to argue that the favors get doled out a little unequally around here, are you?"

Bill chuckled. "No, I'm not going to argue that."

"And regardless of the reason, it's obvious that Mayor Bruce has a certain...bias."

Bill smirked. "And you wouldn't have any bias if you were in office?"

"I think my record with the Chamber of Commerce stands for itself."

Bill seemed to consider this, taking a sip of coffee while he did so.

Mike stepped into the space in the conversation. "Since we're talking about funds for worthy ventures here, Bill, Maxwell could certainly use your financial support. As I'm sure you're aware, running against Mayor Bruce is not an inexpensive undertaking."

Bill chuckled again. "I would imagine not." He turned toward Maxwell, his face harder than it had been throughout the lunch. He'd dropped the guise of friendly farmer and picked up the visage of the prosperous businessman.

"I can appreciate where you're coming from with your ideas and I think they're admirable," Bill said. "I also like the fact that you and your family have been in Oldham for quite a while now. I think your parents opened their inn less than a year after I opened my farm."

Mike leaned toward Bill. "So you'll write us a check?"

Bill took another long sip of his coffee. "There's the elephant in the room, Mike."

Maxwell had no idea what Bill was talking about, and he could see that Mike was equally perplexed.

"Elephant?" Mike said.

"The poll numbers. You didn't think I'd come to this lunch without checking on where things stood, did you?" He glanced slowly from Mike to Maxwell. "The numbers are going in the wrong direction, gentlemen."

Maxwell felt his gut tighten. Until this moment, he hadn't considered the effect the latest numbers could have on fundraising, which was a ridiculous oversight on his part.

Mike held out a hand. "That's why we need your help, Bill. Mayor Bruce is grossly outspending us right now. If we don't get assistance from people like you, he's going to buy himself another term of office without any fair competition."

Bill appeared to consider this for a few seconds. "I can appreciate that, Mike. Truly I can. Here's the thing, though: I can't afford to make an enemy out of the mayor if it looks like he's going to continue to be the mayor. I've been the beneficiary of those development funds on more than one occasion. It wouldn't be good for me if those grants stopped coming."

Maxwell could hardly believe what Bill was saying. Valley Farms was hugely profitable. The last thing Bill needed was a grant from the town. In fact, it was difficult to imagine how he even qualified for a grant. This was clearly a case of the rich getting richer at the expense of so many others who needed the money more. Yet another thing to change if he ever got his chance.

Maxwell found it impossible to participate in the conversation any longer. Mike continued to spin and Bill continued to demur, but Maxwell could see that this was a lost cause. Bill Nelson wasn't going to be contributing to the campaign. In fact, Maxwell had the feeling that Bill Nelson might become an adversary in the near future.

He wanted to believe that the situation with Bill was particular to Bill. Many of the town's most successful businesspeople were more civically minded than the farmer. Would they be any more willing to back him, though, if the general perception was that he was running a losing campaign?

If Mike and Maxwell didn't find a way to regain momentum, it was entirely possible that no new big donors would be coming on board.

~⌣

Maxwell and Maria had been having coffee together once a week since Maxwell returned to Oldham more than a decade ago. It was a way for brother and sister to stay in touch away from the constant swirl of activity that was present whenever the entire family got together, a way of having a visit rather than participating in an event. Seeing each other when everyone else was around had been a treasured experience for a long time — Gold family dinners would always have a distinctive place in Maxwell's heart — but there was rarely time to talk about anything of substance. That's what these gatherings were for.

"So how's my beautiful nephew doing?" Maria said. "You know he might just be the second cutest person in the entire Gold family."

Maxwell assumed that she was putting Joey behind her college-age daughter Olivia and not someone else in the clan, like herself.

"He's going a million miles an hour, as usual. Still pin-balling off of everything in his path. He hasn't broken anything this week, so that's some kind of progress."

"Good thing he's built of study stock."

Maxwell laughed. "Yes it is. He's taken some falls that I thought would lay him out, maybe even send him to the hospital, but he always just bounces back up."

Maria smiled and looked off in the middle distance, which gave Maxwell a moment to focus on his thoughts about his son. Joey did seem to get hurt more than the average three-year-old, but he also seemed to be remarkably resilient. Did that resilience come with a price, though? Were some of his recent issues related to the fact that he always seemed to be picking himself off the ground?

"He's doing some weird stuff lately," Maxwell said, his tone changing.

Maria's eyes reconnected with his. "What do you mean?"

"He's having some odd behavioral issues. Breaking down in tears for no reason, acting defiantly, testing my patience."

Maria shrugged. "Isn't that standard stuff for a kid his age?"

"It hasn't been standard stuff for Joey. I'm not saying he was always the most stable child in the world, but he didn't start doing any of this stuff until a few months ago.

And it seems to be ramping up. We've had some real howlers lately — and I mean that literally."

Maria seemed to give this a moment's thought and then said, "I wouldn't worry about it. Olivia went through a stage around this age when she liked dropping things just to see what would happen. We lost a vase that had been in Doug's family for generations because of this. There was a little stretch where I thought this might be symptomatic of something else."

"And then what happened?"

"Nothing. She just stopped doing it. I guess it stopped being entertaining."

Maxwell wasn't at all sure this was the same kind of thing, but he didn't want to alarm his sister by going into further detail about some of Joey's breakdowns and the duration of them. This could very well be a stage Joey was going through, and making more of an issue of it with Maria now might cause her to develop the wrong impression of her nephew. You always had to be careful of that with family. You make a huge issue about something, it works itself out and you forget about it, but those you confided in don't.

He decided to veer from the topic. "He discovered *Rocky and Bullwinkle* the other day, which made me irrationally happy."

Maria grinned. "I never understood what you saw in that cartoon."

"And yet I still love you, sis, even though your taste in pop culture is suspect."

"I introduced you to nearly all of your favorite music!"

Maxwell raised his hands. "Okay, fair point. But do you still watch reality TV?"

"You can't paint all reality television with the same brush."

"Let me ask the question a different way. Are you still watching those shows where the women spend the entire hour saying miserable things about each other?"

Maria looked down at the table. "They're funny."

Maxwell leaned back in his chair. "Now I understand why you don't like *Rocky and Bullwinkle*. The show is too nuanced."

Maria reached for a sugar packet and threw it at Maxwell, missing him by several feet.

"Okay, I get why it would be fun to share that with Joey," she said. "I remember when Olivia expressed an interest in The Indigo Girls. She'd ask me to play 'Galileo' over and over again. I just loved it." She sipped her coffee and looked off in the middle distance again. When she spoke, her voice was wistful. "I miss having a little kid in the house."

"Hey, you're still young. Maybe you should get pregnant again."

Maria's expression went from wistful to sarcastic. "I'm not sure who would kill me first — Doug or Olivia."

Maxwell guessed it would be Doug. His brother-in-law had made no secret of how much he enjoyed being an empty-nester in his early forties, even though he adored his daughter. Maria, on the other hand, still seemed to be struggling with the adjustment, in spite of the fact that she was once again writing and performing music with a passion she hadn't exhibited in a couple of decades.

Maxwell wondered if the roles would be reversed in his household. Though it was a very long time away, maybe Annie would be the one to celebrate the freedom afforded by Joey's going off to college while Maxwell pined over the loss. He could definitely see that happening, especially his part in it.

The thought gave him an idea.

"Maybe you could rent one."

Maria's eyebrows arched.

"Well, 'rent' is the wrong word. Maybe you can borrow one. For a weekend. Soon."

Maria rolled her eyes. "Are you asking me to babysit?"

"I was suggesting I do you the favor of lending you my son for a couple of days to ease the ache in your heart."

Maria tipped her head toward him. "You're asking me to babysit so you and Annie can get away, right?"

"Yeah, that's exactly what I'm asking. That would be an *incredible* blessing."

"A little second honeymoon action?"

The idea had only just come to Maxwell, so he wasn't sure exactly what he had in mind. Someone had advised him many years ago that it was unwise to involve family in one's marital troubles and that seemed like good counsel right now. The advice hadn't meant much to Maxwell at the time because, pre-Joey, things had always been great with Annie. However, when that stopped being true, he never thought to confide in his siblings. That meant that Maria was unaware of what was going on in his household — she didn't even know about Annie's three-day disappearance — and it seemed like a good idea to keep it that way. Still, he wasn't revealing anything by making this request of his sister.

Second honeymoon? Maxwell thought back to the trip to Costa Rica Annie and he had taken after their wedding. Their hunger for each other was palpable, even though they'd been living together for a couple of years and had known each other since high school. A switch just seemed to be activated on their wedding day, as if this new level of commitment unlocked another level of intimacy. Could he hope for even a hint of that now with a weekend away?

"One night in a B&B would be very, very welcome," he said. "You have no idea how much of a challenge it is to get any time alone."

Maria grinned. "So there might be some upside for you in doing this *favor* for me."

"Yeah, a little one, maybe. But you'd be getting Joey."

"So it's a win-win."

"Exactly."

Maria sat back in her seat and brought her coffee cup to her lips. She drank slowly and then said, "Pick a weekend."

Chapter 3

~

From the Port waiting for you on your arrival to the Egyptian cotton bedding to Mary Ann's maple pecan pancakes or roasted eggplant chorizo frittata when you wake up, we have designed everything at the River's Turn Inn around your comfort and enjoyment. Take a break from the pace of your everyday lives and let us take care of you for a while.

Maxwell had been browsing bed-and-breakfast websites since putting Joey to bed. There were certain parameters to his search; for example, he didn't want to be more than two hours from home and he didn't want to stay in a place with more than a dozen rooms. A full breakfast in the morning was a must, because the "breakfast" part of "bed and breakfast" was, in his opinion, far more important than the "bed" part. Beyond that, he would explore the many options available.

There was no shortage of choices. Maxwell's parents had maintained a successful inn in Oldham for more than thirty years, doing well enough to support five children and leave them with a small windfall when it was sold. But their success wasn't because of a lack of competition. With the Sugar Maple now in new hands, there were four B&Bs within the confines of Oldham and another dozen within a fifteen-mile radius. Within a two-hour drive, there were literally hundreds. Maxwell had no idea where the accommodations industry ranked in this part of New England, but he guessed that it was in the top ten.

River's Turn sounded special, an assessment confirmed by several consumer-rating sites. The people who didn't like it seemed not to like it for reasons Maxwell would have loved, saying things like, "It was too quiet," "It was too out of the way," and, "The innkeepers insisted on talking to us during breakfast." Maxwell often found that negative consumer comments could be especially helpful in making a decision. If the detractors were clearly not like him, they offered their own sort of endorsement in a the-enemy-of-my-enemy-is-my-friend way. On the other hand, if commenters complained about things that also tended to irk Maxwell, he knew to stay away.

He checked the online reservation system for availability during the first two weekends in September and found that there were rooms available for both. Maxwell doubted that the same would have been true if he'd been searching in October, the height of the season in this area because of the stunning fall foliage. That wasn't particularly meaningful to him, though; by October, he'd be so busy with the campaign that he was likely to have trouble scheduling bathroom breaks. Even getting away in September was going to generate some pushback from Mike, but Maxwell would deal with that; it was too important that he have this alone time with Annie for him to let anything stand in the way.

Happy with the result of his search, he brought his laptop over to the couch where Annie was sitting watching something on television. This was the first night in several that she hadn't been focused on reading a book on her tablet. The show on the screen was in mid-scene and Maxwell knew better than to interrupt. Within a couple of minutes, though, a commercial came on.

"Hey, look at this," he said, handing the laptop to his wife.

Annie took it from him and glanced at the inn's home page, scrolling down a bit. When she didn't comment, Maxwell said, "Doesn't it look great?"

"Um, sure." She scrolled back up to the top of the page. "You're not trying to tell me that you want to buy an inn if you lose the election, are you?"

Maxwell laughed. He'd never once entertained the idea of going into the "family business." He respected his parents' choice of a career, but it held no appeal for him; he knew too much about it. "No, not at all. Wow, definitely not. I was thinking more about a romantic weekend getaway."

Annie tilted her head toward him, eyeing him dubiously. She looked at the computer again and then back at him. "Going someplace like this with Joey in tow is hardly my definition of romantic."

"I'm glad to hear that, though I'm a little dismayed to think that you thought it would have been *my* definition of romantic. This is where it gets really good: Maria volunteered to let Joey stay with her and Doug for a weekend of our choice. It's entirely possible that *I* volunteered *her*, actually, but either way I was definitely thinking of this as an adults-only excursion."

A look of mild surprise flashed across Annie's face and then she quickly went back to the laptop. "Maria hasn't had a toddler in the house for a long time," she said with concern in her voice.

"They say it's like riding a bicycle."

"I'm also not sure Joey's ready for this. You remember what he was like the one time we tried to go away without him."

Maxwell remembered it well. Joey was barely a year old and they were on their way to a friend's wedding in Manhattan when they got a call from Maxwell's mother saying that Joey had started projectile vomiting. They wound up turning around and they spent the time they'd planned to spend dancing at the emergency room.

"I don't think preparedness had anything to do with that. I think the key is avoiding feeding him strawberries." It turned out that Joey had had an extremely severe allergic reaction and there hadn't been a single berry of any kind in the Gold household since then.

"It could happen again."

"It really couldn't. Maria is well aware of the strawberry issue. She's also well aware of the keep-everything-breakable-far-from-sight policy."

Annie stared at the computer screen again, then up at the television when the show came back on. Maxwell guessed that he was going to have to wait for another commercial, but Annie's eyes went back to the laptop.

"How can you even think about a weekend away? Aren't we shackled to Oldham until the campaign is over?"

"Not if I tell Mike I need to take a step back to refresh. This is local politics, not a presidential election. CNN isn't exactly following my every move. As an extra bonus, this place is in Rhode Island, so the odds of running into a constituent are that much smaller."

Annie handed the laptop back to him. "We haven't done anything like this in a long time."

He wasn't sure what that meant to her. Was she saying, "It would be great to do something we haven't done in years," or was she saying, "We don't do this anymore?"

"We're overdue," he said.

Annie stared at the television again, though she didn't seem to be engaging with it. She just seemed to be looking in the direction of the TV. Still, a full fifteen seconds passed before she spoke again.

"Maria's really up for keeping Joey?"

Maxwell moved forward a bit on the couch. "She seemed enthusiastic about it."

"If we went on the weekend, I'd wind up missing my yoga class."

"We'll stretch…among other things."

She turned to him when he said that, and Maxwell thought he caught a hint of surprise on her face.

"When did you want to go?"

Maxwell moved to show Annie the reservation page on the site and then realized this didn't matter to her. "I was thinking the second weekend in September."

She paused again, then said, "Yeah, okay."

Maxwell's spirits surged. He only then realized that he'd been expecting Annie to dismiss this idea. "I can book it?"

"Yeah, okay."

With that, Annie turned back to the television, this time actually seeming to be watching. Maxwell started to get up to take the laptop back to his desk to make the reservation and then just decided he could do the same thing on the couch, where he could stay with his wife.

∿

"Mr. Gold, high school reading and math scores were both down nearly two percent in Oldham this year over last year. Is this an indication that our children are falling behind and, if so, what do you plan to do about it if you become mayor?"

Maxwell's first debate against Mayor Bruce was this Thursday, and his staff was taking him through yet another rigorous prep on likely topics. His campaign strategist Steve was playing the role of Sean Hopper, the newscaster who would be moderating the debate.

"Well, Sean, I think it's important to put those numbers into context. For one thing, a two percent fluctuation wouldn't be a cause for panic under any circumstance. However, in this case, we need to look at the state test scores overall. The state switched to a new testing system this year and every district's numbers took a hit. If you compare our numbers to the rest of Connecticut, you'll see that we declined less than all but three districts in the entire state and considerably less than most."

"That was a good answer," Mike said. He was seated to the right of the podium they'd set up in the conference room to simulate the debate setting, while Steve was positioned directly in front of it.

Steve raised his hand in a stop sign. "It was a good answer, Maxwell, but it also opens you up for a hit from Mayor Bruce. He could say that you're being soft on education and that you're willing to accept a slow decline into mediocrity."

Steve was right. Maxwell had a tendency to assume reasonableness from his opponent — after all, the facts behind the test score decline had been well reported throughout the state — and that was flawed thinking when it came to Bruce. Last week, they reviewed videos of Bruce's debates during the last mayoral campaign, and Maxwell counted at least three sucker punches. He had to go into this assuming that the mayor would seek every opportunity to twist Maxwell's statements, even if there was strong logic behind those statements.

Maxwell nodded his head vigorously. He turned away from the two men in the room for a moment to compose his thoughts and then stepped back to the podium to deliver his different answer.

"Sean, the numbers are a little misleading, because the state is administering new tests and scores are down everywhere. In fact, our students performed very well in comparison to most of the other districts in Connecticut. That said, we never want to ignore a downward trend, even if there's an explanation for it. I'm going to want to work very closely with the superintendent and the entire board of education to make sure that we assess this decline carefully. Given the many ideas I have for progressive changes in our school system, I'm convinced that our children will soon be excelling at this test and every other test the state throws at them."

Steve sent Maxwell a thumbs-up and Maxwell smiled at him before looking over at Mike.

"The first answer was good," the campaign chair said. "The second one was better."

The key, of course, was for Maxwell to give the better answer the first time. On Thursday, he wouldn't get any "do-overs." Bruce wasn't going to offer him any wiggle room, and he couldn't count on softball questions from Hopper, who'd endorsed the incumbent on air during the last election and was nearly certain to do so again.

"Shoot me something on infrastructure," he said to Steve.

Steve skimmed through his notes and then looked up excitedly. He seemed to be enjoying this role, probably wishing he could be in Sean Hopper's seat the night of the debate.

"Mr. Gold, in your position of president of the Chamber of Commerce, you've repeatedly come out against the construction of a multi-level parking garage on Hickory Avenue even though the Vector lot could now be used for this purpose and parking is an ever-increasing problem in the downtown area. Mayor Bruce has advocated leasing the space to a private company for this purpose and said it will be one of the first things he does in his next term if reelected. If you unseat Mayor Bruce, would you continue to oppose this?"

Maxwell groaned inwardly. This parking debate had been going on seemingly forever, though the Vector lot had only recently become a possibility. It was perhaps his least favorite topic during monthly Chamber meetings, and it had already come up several times during the campaign. This was a thorny one, because even some of the people firmly in Maxwell's camp disagreed with him on this issue.

"Sean, there's no simple answer here. I'm sure the mayor understands this, as parking has been a problem throughout each of his terms. The reason I've always opposed a multi-level lot on Hickory Avenue is that no one has ever shown me a plan that avoids diminishing the visual appeal of our main street. Surveys have consistently shown that our residents shop the independent, locally owned stores on Hickory and people come here from other parts of the state and beyond to spend their money because they love the beauty and serenity of this commercial area. Could the Vector lot be the answer? If it's put in the hands of the right architect who is given the right direction, maybe."

Mike came over and patted Maxwell on the shoulder. "Nice job of taking a little swipe at Bruce while you answered that question."

"You know he's going to wind up leasing it to Pinnacle and they'll make it an eyesore," Steve said. "You could throw that in as well, if you want."

Pinnacle Construction was the firm that had been implicated in the scandal surrounding the mayor last fall. Mike's newspaper beat that story to death, but they were never able to prove that Bruce had illegally accepted money in return for favors. Still, polling indicated that a majority of Oldham residents believed that the mayor was at least partially guilty, and in early polls many said that this belief would cause them to consider another candidate for mayor. One could say that Pinnacle Construction was responsible for Maxwell standing where he was today.

Maxwell shook his head. "I thought we agreed on taking the high road."

Steve offered an exaggerated shrug. "Just *mentioning* Pinnacle isn't dirty politics."

"Let's get back to the questions."

They refocused and worked their way through budget issues, traffic, the various concerns of the commercial district, park safety, and more. When Mike finally suggested that they call it a day, Maxwell looked at his phone and saw that more than five hours had passed since they'd started. He hadn't even noticed that the time had melted away. Maxwell regularly had that experience when playing with Joey, and it used to happen with Annie regularly. Other than that, it had been a very long while since something made him so completely lose track of time.

∽

During the real debate that Thursday night, Maxwell was thrilled to discover that the first few questions were right in his wheelhouse. Rather than asking about the test scores, Sean had asked about a middle school over-crowding issue. The mayor talked about split sessions, which would lead to longer days for teachers and create complications for work-ing parents. It was difficult to believe that many people watching the debate — espe-cially anyone who might be affected by such a change — was happy with that answer. During his rebuttal, Maxwell showed that he had given this plenty of thought. He of-fered a solution he believed in strongly: us-ing a vacant technical school adjacent to one of the middle schools to serve as overflow. The mayor challenged him on logistics, but Maxwell was prepared with a plan, one that showed he was more than capable of thinking outside the box to help the community.

The second question was about the ongoing development of the secondary commercial district on Sumac Boulevard. Maxwell could have answered this one in his sleep. As president of the Chamber of Commerce, he was working with these shop owners every day, along with helping commercial realtors with search and recruiting. The question gave him a high-profile opportunity to introduce an idea he'd been developing over the past several months, one that offered incentives to top restaurants in Fairfield County to open satellite restaurants in Oldham. The fact that he could announce the signing of a new restaurant by one of the top chefs in the tri-state area made this seem more like a press conference than a face-off between candidates. Bruce grumbled a rebuttal, and it seemed to Maxwell that the mayor was barely aware of the incoming restaurant, even though all deals of this sort had to go through his office for vetting. Maxwell had won that round easily.

After all of the debate prep and the endless hours spent brushing up on areas where he had a steeper learning curve, Maxwell was amazed with how quickly he found himself in his comfort zone. Mayor Bruce had tried to spar with him, but he'd so far failed to land a blow. Maxwell had never considered himself to be a debating natural, but maybe this was a latent talent just beginning to emerge. Regardless, he was feeling great.

Then things pivoted so quickly that Maxwell thought he might have gotten whiplash.

"Mr. Gold, if you were elected mayor, how would you plan to address the recent suggestion from the town council that the only way to maintain a balanced budget is to raise the mill rate on property taxes?"

Maxwell stole a glance at Mike Mills, which he knew was in itself a strategic mistake. The TV cameras would have caught this, and there was a very good chance that viewers would interpret such a glance as an indication that he wasn't equipped to handle the question on his own. In truth, he wasn't equipped to handle it with Mike's help, either. This was the first he'd heard about any discussion of raising the mill rate. Why hadn't any of his staff brought this up during the numerous pre-debate sessions? Why hadn't Mike, who through his position at the newspaper had access to everyone in and around Oldham, brought it up as a potential bone of contention?

Maxwell knew he couldn't gloss over this question. Property taxes affected nearly every voter in Oldham in some way. If, like him, many of them were only just learning about the possibility of a tax hike, they would be keenly focused on his plan to address this situation, and his answer could affect their decision to vote for him. This was the kind of heightened moment that created impressions that were difficult to revise. If he gave the wrong answer now, many viewers could turn away from him now and not even remember why they'd done so when they went to vote.

Maxwell allowed himself another couple of seconds to pull his thoughts together and then spoke. "There are numerous ways to increase Oldham's revenue, Sean. A property tax hike is only one way, and I'd like to believe we'd explore all available options before settling on that. I would prefer to prioritize the promotion of our local businesses. If our merchants sell more goods, our sales tax revenue could cover any budget shortfall."

Maxwell thought he'd done a decent job of thinking on his feet. He'd managed to offer another way of addressing the matter — one that involved getting in a plug for small business, a key constituency for him — without promising that he wouldn't raise the mill rate.

He felt good about himself for exactly as long as it took Sean to ask Mayor Bruce for a rebuttal.

"What my opponent is suggesting sounds fine until you consider one thing," Bruce said.

"It is completely a fantasy. To make up for our revenue shortfall through sales tax income alone would require our merchants to increase their sales by somewhere around thirty percent over the robust business they already do. That would be a nice trick in a relatively flat economy, and as much faith as I have in our small businesses, I would never want to put that kind of pressure on them.

"Fortunately, my team has been working on a solution ever since our economists made me aware that a problem could be brewing. It's too complex to lay out in detail here, but it involves calling in some markers from Hartford and getting a more equitable share of state revenues. My people and I know how to do this and we *will* do it. The people of Oldham don't need to be concerned about an increase in their property taxes. At least not while my plan is in place."

Maxwell felt as though someone had stuck a pin in him. With that one answer, the mayor had made himself sound like a champion of the people, a friend of Maxwell's greatest group of supporters, and a true insider who knew how to get things done. As a bonus, he'd made Maxwell sound like an amateur who didn't know how government worked. If this were a boxing match, Maxwell might have scored a few points in the first couple of rounds, but Jack Bruce had just laid him on the mat, his mouthpiece lying ten feet behind him.

None of the remainder of the debate was as calamitous as that exchange. Maxwell fumbled a bit on a question about the fire department, and he wasn't particularly pleased with his answer about recycling — which was crazy because he'd been working for months on a way to improve how Oldham recycled. While there were no additional disasters, it was obvious from the way Bruce looked at him when they shook hands at the end that the mayor believed he'd won easily. It was difficult to contest that assertion.

Mike put an arm around Maxwell's shoulders as he walked backstage. "You looked good out there," Mike said.

Maxwell grimaced. "At least I was wearing a nice suit."

Mike moved to stand in front of him. "You were very strong on a number of the issues."

Maxwell looked down at the ground and then back up at Mike. "He killed me with that tax question."

Mike nodded slowly. "He did kill you with that."

Maxwell wasn't expecting an argument from Mike on the topic, but his campaign manager could have at least pretended to offer one. "How badly did I hurt us tonight?"

"You didn't hurt us. At worst you didn't gain ground."

"Which is a problem, since I'm currently behind."

"It would be much more of a problem if this were the end of October rather than the end of August. We have two more debates to go, and Bruce will probably have three more scandals between now and then."

Maxwell chuckled at that. Mike had never been shy about questioning the mayor's ethics. It felt good to laugh about something given how unhappy he was with himself.

"We'll get back at it tomorrow afternoon," Mike said.

Maxwell agreed and shook Mike's hand. Then he was off to speak with the media while Mike did some spinning with influencers. If he was lucky, they'd be out of the auditorium in a half hour. Maxwell was looking forward to getting home and kissing his (hopefully) sleeping son. Then he'd find out what Annie thought of the debate. Assuming she watched it. Mayor Bruce's wife was of course up on the stage kissing him after they finished. The two of them never missed a photo opportunity. Maxwell had told the press ahead of time that Annie was going to be home taking care of their young son. It seemed to work for now, but Maxwell wondered how long that would continue to be the case.

In a couple of months, it might not matter.

Chapter 4

The River's Turn Inn really was as refined and comfortable as advertised. The innkeepers were friendly, the Port they served in the afternoon was vintage and from a small bottling, the room was both quaint and elegant, and the bed was luxurious with a memory foam mattress and high-quality linens. The accommodations were everything Maxwell could have hoped for. This made it especially unfortunate that he was lying in bed at 7:45 on Sunday morning in a funk.

He and Annie had had a good day yesterday, one of the most relaxed they'd experienced together in a couple of years. Right from the start, it seemed that fate was tilting in their favor. They'd dropped Joey at Maria's a little after ten and he'd immediately begun playing with a guitar Maria had bought her daughter Olivia when she was Joey's age. It was so smart of Maria to have a "special toy" for him when he entered the house. Annie had been concerned that Joey might give them a hard time about their going away, but he just kissed them both and got back to his "music."

There was very little traffic on the drive up to the inn, and they kept the conversation light while listening to Annie's R.E.M. Pandora station on the car stereo. When they got to The River's Turn, they put their bag up in their room and then walked through a surprisingly busy town, getting lunch at a natural foods place and then browsing craft shops and boutiques. Maxwell bought Annie a beautiful hand-knit scarf at one store, and she reciprocated by buying him a handmade ceramic coffee mug at another. After Port and a nap back at the inn, they went to dinner at a farm-to-table restaurant about twenty minutes away that Deborah, Maxwell's chef sister, recommended. The meal lasted nearly three hours and concluded with one of the best salted-caramel bread puddings Maxwell had ever eaten. Meanwhile, Maxwell was concerned that they'd spend the night talking about Joey while he avoided mentioning the campaign, but they touched on many things, from a high school classmate of theirs Annie had recently reconnected with on Facebook, to a movie they had watched together the other night, to even an imitation Annie did of the mayor's wife. The change of venue seemed to lift Annie's spirits, and he saw parts of her personality — the ebullient, optimistic parts — that he hadn't seen much of late.

Maxwell was feeling quite serene by the time they got back to the inn, much less because of the bottle of Rioja they'd shared and much more because of how simply everything seemed to be flowing. As was often the case when he was feeling serene — when the clamoring in his head about work or campaigns or child rearing was quieted — he was also feeling amorous. Prior to Joey's arrival, Maxwell and Annie had had an extremely active and creative sex life. Maxwell didn't have a great deal of experience with women before Annie, but he had enough to know that she was an unusually affectionate and playful lover. Making love with Annie was always warm and fulfilling, as much about the connection as the sensation — though the sensation was spectacular. Maxwell had once read that truly committed sex was the ultimate form of meditation, the ultimate communion with a higher plane, and for most of his relationship with Annie, he knew exactly what that meant. He didn't only find pleasure when Annie and he made love; he also found peace.

Since Joey, though, sex between Maxwell and Annie seemed mostly about release. Where it was once fairly common for them to make love four or five times a week, it was now surprising if they did so more than once or twice a month, and even when they did Annie rarely seemed to be in the same place with him. Every now and then, they would lock eyes when they were entwined and Maxwell would feel the eternal feeling he used to get regularly when they were together. Now, though, it happened so infrequently that he'd begun to wonder if he'd always been imagining it or at the very least given it a meaning that wasn't really there.

While Maxwell hadn't specifically arranged this getaway to have sex with his wife, it was definitely something he'd planned on. He was hoping that their being away from any possibility of Joey awakening and disturbing them would allow them to take the time for the luxurious exploration of each other that had once been an essential component of their lovemaking. If they just had a nice, long unfettered stretch together, maybe they could reconnect at that eternal level and maybe this would travel back with them to Oldham, at least in part.

When they got back to the room, Maxwell pulled Annie into his arms. She stayed there for a long moment and Maxwell reveled in the closeness of her. But then she pulled back and said, "Let's get ready for bed," turning to go into the bathroom. They washed up and brushed teeth as though it was an average weekday night. Then, when they got between the sheets, Annie commented on how comfortable the bed was — the same thing she said when they'd napped on it earlier — and Maxwell moved onto his side to embrace her again. As before, Annie snuggled into him, but nothing ever progressed from there. There was no chance that she didn't understand his intent; he rubbed her back and then feathered her neck with his fingernails as he always did as a prelude to lovemaking, but Annie just stayed pressed against him. They remained like this for maybe twenty minutes before Annie said, "This was a nice night," kissed him, and turned away from him.

This left Maxwell completely baffled. He couldn't possibly have missed some expression of upset or anger on Annie's part. She hadn't been reticent all day — they even held hands during dinner. And once they'd been in bed, nothing happened that might have caused her to back away from him, at least nothing he could identify.

Annie nodded off within seconds of turning over, which made her considerably more fortunate than he. It took Maxwell the longest time to get to sleep after she did. All he could do was recap the day, looking for some sign that he might have missed.

He eventually nodded off, but he awoke early in the morning and picked up the conversation he'd been having with himself before he slumbered. Soon, this evolved into a review of the last three years of their marriage. There had been some major blowups, of course, punctuated by Annie's disappearance from the family for a few days last fall, but the more insidious erosion wasn't marked by anything so dramatic. Instead, it could be identified by juxtaposing a picture of them taking Joey home from the hospital and one from any recent moment, say his arrival from work Friday night. Two days after Joey was born, Maxwell was entirely convinced that he and Annie shared the same dreams, the same vision of family, and the same unwavering sense of their union. He'd be kidding himself if he said that he believed the same thing now. Annie had made it clear to Maxwell that his dreams were not hers while simultaneously managing to avoid giving him any idea of what hers had become. Maxwell had no doubt that Annie loved her son absolutely, but she also considered Joey to be a burden, something Maxwell never thought, even on the most difficult nights. And as far as their being a unit, all he had to do was go back to the end of last night to see how out of sync they'd become.

Annie started to stir. It was early for her to awaken without being prompted to do so by a toddler, and Maxwell fully expected her to shift a bit and go back to sleep. Instead, she turned toward him.

"What time is it?" she said.

Maxwell looked at the clock on the nightstand next to him. "It's eight-oh-three."

She moved closer to him and Maxwell instinctually put his arm around her.

Annie threw an arm across his chest. "You were awake, right?"

"Yeah, I got up a little while ago."

She nuzzled closer, and he thought he felt a kiss on his chest. "How late did they say they were serving breakfast?"

"I'm pretty sure she said ten."

Annie snuggled even tighter and began to rub his arm lightly. "So we have time?"

Was she saying what he thought she was saying?

"Yeah, it's early."

Annie shifted her body so that she was mostly lying on top of him. "That's good."

Maxwell began to react to this instantly. He had never once been able to deny his attraction to Annie and he wasn't going to start this morning. He pulled her toward him and kissed her at first slowly and then with increasing passion.

At some point, he was going to have to try to make sense of this weekend. That point wasn't now, though.

Chapter 5

$\sim$

It didn't happen often, but there were definitely times during Chamber of Commerce meetings when Maxwell wished he could simply go back to bed. Reboot the day and see if he could get it to work more efficiently. The current conversation about signage on Birch Boulevard — a conversation that had now extended beyond a half-hour — was one of those instances.

As president of the Chamber, it was impolitic for Maxwell to say many of the things that would run through his head during this recurring debate. Things like, "Business on Birch is awful; wouldn't *anything* be better?" or "Putting up a bigger sign isn't going to hide the fact that Naylor's Hardware looks like it hasn't seen a coat of paint since the fifties." There were underlying problems with the commercial district on Birch that were never going to be addressed with a few cosmetic changes. Maxwell had tried to attend to these problems with the shop owners there for several years now. Instead, the merchants chose to pursue quick fixes, such as asking for a variance on the city's signage laws. As though unwilling to offer any hope of survival to the "runt of the litter," the other members of the Chamber hung tight to the regulations as though all of Oldham was going to be diminished if the merchants on Birch were allowed to try to attract customers with gaudy displays.

This conversation had essentially brought the meeting to a halt. This was unfortunate, because prior to the signage discussion, things had been moving along at a nice pace and there was an air of opportunity in the room. After some tight years, business was up in most sectors in Oldham and there was a strong sense of optimism for business overall as the city entered into one of the most important periods of the year. There seemed to be an abundance of good ideas floating around the Oldham business community, and Maxwell was proud of the fact that he'd incubated several of them. His restaurant initiative was gaining traction, and his introduction of the Sunday open-air market on the east side of town had not only been a smash for those who participated, but also a boon to the businesses in the vicinity.

Maxwell always found that he needed to walk a thin line when meetings descended into looping debate. Tabling the discussion was likely to anger those engaged in it, but all he needed to do was look around the room to see that those not involved in the conversation — the majority of those in attendance — were losing patience, checking their cellphones and signaling with their body language that they believed their time was being wasted. Whether it was politic or not, he needed to step in.

"I think we've heard good arguments on both sides of this conversation," he said. "I think it's also fair to say that we haven't heard any *new* arguments on either side. We've been batting this around for the past three months without ever getting to the point of action. I therefore motion that we agree to vote on the variance at next month's meeting. Do I have a second?"

Several people around the table leapt at the opportunity to second the motion. Maxwell noticed that most of them were members who had not participated in the debate.

"We'll add the vote to the agenda for our next meeting then. Any documents members would like to submit for consideration before the vote will need to be submitted one week prior."

Maxwell looked down at his agenda for the current meeting. "That concludes our old business. Would anyone like to introduce any new business?"

No one in the room stirred. Maxwell expected as much. Even the signage combatants were worn out, and everyone really needed to get back to work.

"Okay, then I'm going to call this meeting to a close. Thank you, all."

The room emptied quickly. Even Mike Mills, who usually hung back to offer snarky commentary on the proceedings left with just a wave. As he always did, Maxwell stayed in the conference room to jot down a few notes before going back to his office. He expected to be alone when he looked up, but instead he found a striking woman who seemed to be in her early forties standing about fifteen feet away. She smiled at him when they made eye contact.

"Hi," he said, feeling a tiny bit odd that he hadn't felt the woman's presence while he was writing.

She moved toward him and offered her hand. "We haven't met. I'm Alecia Moore. I opened Moore is More Party Planning about six months ago."

Maxwell had heard about the operation. From what he knew, Alecia Moore was something of a big deal in Boston, having built her party planning enterprise into a major player in that city before deciding to relocate here. Why anyone in her business would choose to move from a city of six hundred thousand to one of sixty thousand was a mystery to him, but he hadn't been curious enough to find out. It was the kind of thing he would have done automatically in the pre-campaign days. Thinking of that gave him the tiniest twinge of guilt. He knew he was taking care of his responsibilities at the Chamber, but doing his job was overwhelmingly different from doing his best.

He shook her hand. "It's nice to meet you, Alecia. I hope Oldham has been treating you well so far."

"It has been a revelation in many ways, nearly all of them positive."

"You're not here to tell me that you're unhappy with the size of your sign, are you?"

She smiled at that point, which made her appear even more striking. With closely cropped blonde hair and cobalt-blue eyes, Alecia sent off electric sparks when she brightened. "No, no. I'm not here to lobby you at all. I just wanted to let you know that I found the way you handled that discussion impressive."

Maxwell's eyes widened. "Really? I was guessing that most of the people in the room wanted to have me hanged for letting the conversation go on so long."

She gestured with her hands. "It was the right thing to do."

"You only say that because you haven't been here to witness the same discussion the past three months."

"Actually, I was."

This surprised Maxwell. He found it difficult to believe that he hadn't noticed someone new in the room, let alone someone who looked like Alecia. At the same time, he hadn't noticed her today, either, until she came up to him. Maybe he really was being less conscientious about his work than he thought.

"Sorry," he said.

"Don't be. There are a lot of people sitting at that table every month and you have a lot on your plate. Anyway, I just wanted to say that I thought you were very effective in navigating through that situation, especially since both sides were so obviously dug in."

"Thanks."

"You're going to make a very good mayor."

Maxwell scoffed before he could stop himself. "The poll numbers would disagree with you."

"Well, that's another thing I'd like to discuss with you."

Maxwell arched his eyebrows but didn't say anything.

Alecia continued. "I pride myself on making things happen, connecting dots, creating coalitions."

"Do you get a lot of call for coalition-building in the party business?"

"More than you'd imagine. Also, the party business wasn't the first thing I ever did. Anyway, I'd like to sign on to the campaign to elect Maxwell Gold mayor. I think I can help you build your base."

Maxwell wasn't sure how someone so new to Oldham could help him build his base within Oldham, but maybe an outside perspective was exactly what his campaign needed.

"Do you have time for a cup of coffee?" he said.

∿

"I think she might actually be able to help," Maxwell said as he twirled some spaghetti for his son and handed him the fork. Joey predictably got sauce on the side of his face before the food made it into his mouth. "I mean, Bruce's campaign would probably have a field day with it if they learned that we're using a party planner to build our following, but she really seems to know how to make connections. She used social media terms I'd never heard before."

Maxwell twirled a forkful of spaghetti for himself. This was the way it worked whenever they had pasta — a forkful for his son and then a forkful for him. They'd tried other pastas, but Joey only wanted spaghetti. Maxwell guessed this ritual was at least part of the reason.

"Is she going to have you giving speeches at weddings and sweet sixteens?" Annie said with one eyebrow raised. That particular expression meant that she was saying this to tweak him, not to be playful with him.

"We didn't discuss it," he said nonchalantly. "I'll suggest it to her."

"At least now I know what you'll be doing on the weekends between now and November."

Maxwell's first thought was to suggest to Annie that he couldn't book his weekends too heavily because he never knew when she was going to disappear again for multiple hours without letting him know where she was. He swallowed that, though. Since they'd gotten back from their weekend away, he found himself holding back quite a bit. This wasn't at all what he'd hoped the aftereffect of that trip would be, but it was coming to him increasingly naturally.

It started right after they got out of bed on Sunday morning. In truth, it probably started while they were making love. He could swear he felt himself pulling back from Annie even as they were intertwined. Nothing precipitated it, at least nothing conscious. Maybe it had something to do with the way she'd dismissed him the night before. Maybe it had something to do with the fact that she seemed far more interested in her personal pleasure than in their union. Maybe it was something deeper than even that. Regardless, midway through, he found that he was no longer entirely there. He couldn't remember ever feeling that way before.

"Anyway," he said, "I thought you'd want to know about this. With the tools she's talking about using, it seemed at least a little bit promising."

Annie held up a forkful of pasta. "Too bad your definition of 'promising' and mine are so different."

That seemed a step beyond the cold war they'd been waging over the campaign that extended much further back than their after-sex distance that Sunday morning. Maxwell felt its sting. He twirled another forkful of spaghetti for Joey and tried to let the comment go. This time, he couldn't.

"Can I ask you to do me one favor, Annie? Do you think you could not go to the polls on Election Day? At least that'll be one less vote for Bruce."

Annie seemed surprised by the bitterness in Maxwell's voice. Still, she seemed ready to volley back. This time, though, she didn't get the chance.

"I need potty!" Joey said, jumping out of his chair.

They were at a critical stage in their son's toilet training. Joey was still having accidents on occasion, but he'd gotten considerably better about recognizing his body's signals. However, when he needed to get to a bathroom, it was essential to get him there as quickly as possible.

Maxwell moved his chair back to get up. He was on potty duty whenever he was home.

Joey stamped his feet. "No, Mommy!"

Maxwell continued to get up. "I've got you, Joe. Let Mommy rest." How many times had he said "Let Mommy rest" over the past three years?

Joey ran to his mother's side and started pulling on her arm. "I want Mommy!"

Maxwell could read the annoyance on Annie's face. He reached out a hand to his son. "Joey, come on. You're doing a great job with this. You don't want to have an accident."

Joey tugged harder on Annie. "Mommy take me!"

Maxwell walked toward his son. The idea of wrenching Joey from his mother and then plopping him on the toilet wasn't the kind of imprint he wanted the kid to have of the toilet training experience, but that seemed to be how this was playing out.

As Maxwell got closer, though, Annie stood, rolling her eyes at him.

"Forget it, Maxwell, I'll take him."

With that, she whisked Joey up in her arms, pivoted, and headed toward the bathroom outside of Joey's room.

Leaving Maxwell to wonder what had just happened. Joey *never* rejected him; he always wanted Maxwell to do everything with him. Maxwell was certainly feeling rejected now, though, and this made him feel extremely uncomfortable. It was one thing for matters to be chilly with Annie. If Joey started to marginalize him, though, Maxwell wasn't sure how he would handle it.

I'm overreacting, he thought. *There are times when kids just need their moms. Maybe this is one of those times.*

A few minutes later, Joey and Annie were back. Annie rolled her eyes at him again, but Joey sat back in his chair as though the day had just started over.

"Good pee," he said, meaning he'd held off urinating until he made it to the bathroom. Joey's term, not theirs.

Joey picked up his fork and handed it to Maxwell. "Twirl?"

Maxwell took the fork and gladly twirled spaghetti onto it, relieved that the boy hadn't

decided to choose his mother for this task as
well.

∿

Mike Mills had called exactly one emergency meeting since the campaign had started.
It was in early May, and their lawyers had
thrown a scare into him about the rules of
campaign funding. As he, Maxwell, and the
rest of the staff talked everything through, it
was obvious that Mike came to realize that
there was no cause for concern and that
he felt a bit guilty about raising the alarm.
He vowed never to call another emergency
meeting unless it was a genuine emergency.
And he hadn't called another. Until today.

Maxwell had wall-to-wall meetings scheduled at the Chamber. It was always like that
during the run-up to the fall because of how
important the fall season was to local businesses. Rescheduling a couple of these was
only going to make the rest of the week more
hectic, but Mike had made it clear that a gathering of the key campaign staff was essential
— and that most definitely included the candidate. Maxwell had no idea what had gotten Mike so riled. There wouldn't be another
poll for a couple of weeks, so it couldn't have
anything to do with the numbers. If they'd

gotten a big donor, Mike would have phrased his call for a meeting differently. If they'd *lost* a donor, Mike would have told Maxwell privately before bringing the staff into it. It was a mystery, but one with a definite shelf life. He'd find out soon enough.

Maxwell arrived at the campaign headquarters and waved to Mike, who was walking toward his office.

"They're gathering in the conference room," Mike said. "I just need two minutes."

With that, he went into his office and closed his door. Maxwell couldn't recall Mike ever closing his door to him before. Curious, he shrugged and headed to the conference room. Seated there already were Steve Jordan and Cynthia Robinson. Maxwell grabbed a cup of coffee and then sat at one end of the table.

"I don't suppose either of you have any idea what we're doing here," he said.

Cynthia shook her head slowly.

Steve readjusted himself in his chair. "No idea, which is a little weird. Mike only got here himself a few minutes ago."

The three of them turned as Alecia entered the room. Alecia had proven her worth to Mike very quickly, using a social media platform Maxwell had never heard of before to get a whispering campaign going among people perceived to be undecided voters.

With that, Mike welcomed her onto the team. Maxwell was glad things had turned out that way, because he found Alecia's attitude invigorating.

Alecia sat to Maxwell's right. "There's nothing trending in the blogosphere that is even remotely related to the campaign, so whatever Mike wants to talk to us about, it hasn't gone public."

Maxwell sipped his coffee and tried to get his mind off wondering. He thought about the last meeting he'd had at the Chamber before coming here. It appeared that The Aural Source was going to be closing its doors after more than thirty years. At one time, the store was one of the finest outlets for high-end audio equipment in the area, but Internet retail had cut deeply into its business. When the owner died a year-and-a-half ago, his middle son tried to keep the store alive and current, but it just kept losing money. Maxwell and the son had been reviewing some last-ditch efforts, but none of them were panning out.

A minute or so later, one of the interns popped her head into the conference room, saying, "Oh, good; you're all here" before going out, presumably to inform Mike.

He wants to make an entrance, Maxwell realized. Mike was, after all, a newspaperman, even if the paper itself was rather small-time. He supposed everyone in the newspaper business had at least a bit of a the-atrical streak, a belief that any moment could turn out to be their Woodward-and-Bernstein moment.

Mike came into the conference room at that point, sitting at the opposite end of the table from Maxwell.

"We just received an incredible gift from Mayor Bruce," he said. "He's at it again."

Even if Maxwell didn't know what "at it" meant — which he did — he would have known simply from the gleam in Mike's eyes that the mayor had gotten himself caught up in another scandal.

"Tell me there's something other than payoffs involved this time," Steve said. "Some sex, maybe?"

"Sorry to let you down, Steve, but no sex. It unfortunately appears that the mayor and his wife truly do have a healthy marriage. What we do have, though, is illegal hiring practices — several instances of them — all of which connect directly to Bruce. There's a very clear trail showing that he's been trad-ing jobs for favors."

Steve and Cynthia reacted as excited-ly to this as if Mike had told them that the mayor was sleeping with his secretary while smoking crack. Maxwell glanced over at Ale-cia to gauge her reaction and saw that she didn't seem nearly as energized by this as the others.

Over the next several minutes, Mike laid out the evidence one of his investigative reporters had dug up: indications that Bruce had hired people in exchange for under-the-table agreements with contractors, creditors, and even state government officials. Mike was truly in his element while presenting this; if the newspaper business ever dried up for him, he had a future in daytime television.

Maxwell listened to the conversation, but didn't participate. Mike seemed to think this was the break they'd been waiting for, but Maxwell wasn't sure how it would work in their favor. Bruce had been involved in numerous scandals before. As the polls reinforced repeatedly, most of Oldham had an unfavorable opinion of the mayor's ethics. This hadn't stopped the majority of them from voting for him in the past. Then there was the matter of what Steve had joked about when Mike came into the room: people just seemed bored by this sort of corruption. Sex and drugs were fascinating. So was domestic violence. Even thuggishness captured the imagination. Jobs for favors? It wouldn't come up at the dinner table.

Most important, though, was the fact that Maxwell didn't want to lead the charge in capitalizing on this. He had no trouble with

calling the mayor out for his mistakes in office or areas of policy where the mayor and
Maxwell differed, but he just didn't want to
get into a battle over character. If Maxwell
was going to win, he wanted to do it because
the citizens of Oldham wanted *him*, not because he'd helped cast his opponent in an un-
flattering light.

Steve, Cynthia, and Mike had begun to
strategize ways to get the biggest hit from
this. As they started to talk about press re-
leases and announcements, Maxwell held up
a hand.

"I want to think this through for a couple
of days."

Mike looked at him as though he'd just
said that he wanted to take a trip to Mars
before deciding on action. "What's to think
about? This material has all been vetted."

Maxwell nodded in acknowledgment. "I
still want to think about it."

Mike locked eyes with him for a long moment and it appeared as though he was going
to push back. Instead, he thanked everyone
for coming in and suggested they reconvene
about this at the end of the week. He then
got up to leave, locking eyes with Maxwell
one more time before he did so.

Less than a minute later, Steve and Cynthia left, Steve looking particularly deflated.

"That was the right move," Alecia said.

Maxwell nodded thanks. "I just don't want to get into this garbage."

"*For* you, not *against* him — that's what we're going for."

Maxwell held his hands outward. "Exactly."

"I get it." She looked down at her iPad and swiped it a few times. "I'm glad you do, too." She closed the tablet's cover. "I'll give you a call later. I have a video thing I want to run past you."

She left at that point and Maxwell reviewed all of the activity of the past few minutes. He thought about going to see Mike before heading back to the Chamber offices. Maxwell had obviously ruffled his campaign manager, and it would probably be a good idea to make sure he wasn't too upset. He decided against it, though. Maybe leaving Mike upset at this juncture sent the more important message.

Chapter 6

∼

Maxwell was accustomed to unpredict-able changes to his schedule. Between the rigors of his position at the Chamber and the intensity of the mayoral campaign, he half expected every day to explode in a cacophony of last minute juggling, shoe-horned extra sessions, and pushed-back arrivals home. However, it was a rare case indeed when his schedule was unpredictably *light*. In a surprise confluence, though, both of his afternoon meetings — including one for which he'd set aside two-and-a-half hours — wound up being rescheduled. It was 2:45 in the afternoon, and the rest of his day was clear. It was as though someone had orches-trated an impromptu party,

There was paperwork to do, of course, and projects he'd set aside on multiple occa-sions because of other stresses to his time. He could easily fill the afternoon simply taking care of details that would at some point need to be addressed. However, he also knew that there was much more to gain from taking the opportunity to leave the office early. How many times, especially since the campaign began, had he had to call Annie to say that he'd be late for dinner or that he wasn't going to be coming home for dinner at all? It was time to balance that even a tiny bit by grabbing a surprise extra few hours with his family.

This might prove to be very useful just about now. Things had continued to be cool with Annie in the aftermath of what was supposed to be a romantic getaway. What did it say that an effort to warm things between them managed to make them frostier instead? Meanwhile, Joey continued to go nuclear at a moment's notice. Perhaps breaking up the pattern would be helpful. The weather was beautiful with hints of early fall; maybe they could do something fun outside and then grab dinner at a clam shack or get a sidewalk table someplace. Just the thought of it drove Maxwell to grab his suit jacket and head out of his office.

He informed his assistant that he was disappearing for the day and he thumbed off his work phone before he'd even gotten to the elevator. Mike had his personal cell, of course, as did a few of the more influential Chamber members, so closing the work cell didn't guarantee that business wouldn't intrude on the rest of the day. It did, however, greatly increase the odds.

He didn't think about the possibility that Annie and Joey could be out of the house until he was already in his car and heading home. He hoped that wouldn't be the case. Not only would that scuttle his plan for this free afternoon, but it would also put him in the position of having nothing to do with his time at home. Maxwell really hadn't thought about this until now, but he had very little to do to entertain himself at home if his wife and son weren't there. Between work, parenting, and whatever husband-wife time he could grab, there was no room for avocations. Maybe that would change in the coming months. If he lost to Mayor Bruce — and that was a distinct possibility at this point — he'd get back the time he'd budgeted to the considerable civic duties associated with the position. Meanwhile, meltdowns aside, Joey was growing increasingly independent. He didn't require the full-time monitoring that he had when he first got on his feet, and it was entirely possible that by Christmastime the boy would actually crave some stretches alone, even when Maxwell was around. What would Maxwell do if he suddenly found himself with chunks of free time? In the pre-Joey days, he and Annie had joint pursuits like home improvements, exploring nearby towns, or going to movies or concerts. It wouldn't be as easy for them to use their free time together now, though. For one thing, one of them would still need to be on Joey-duty for the next several years. The boy might be able to be alone in the living room now, but it would be another decade before he could be alone in the house.

And then there was the matter of desire.

Maxwell had been avoiding focusing too closely on this thought, but the reality was that he didn't seem to be a high-priority attraction for his wife anymore. Pre-Joey, if their jobs commandeered too much of their time, Annie would speak longingly about grabbing moments when they could be alone together. She had always made it abundantly clear to him that she cherished their time together, that there was nothing that could substitute for it. Now, he wasn't sure that being with him was even in her top ten of things to do with a free day. If he'd simply said to her, "Maria's taking Joey a few weekends from now, what do you want to do?" would she have suggested a night at a bed-and-breakfast? That was difficult to imagine.

To be honest, though, Maxwell wasn't sure where Annie ranked on his list, either. Until their last night away, he would have said confidently that she was at the very top. That was, after all, why he arranged that brief trip. He couldn't let go of how she nudged him aside that night, though. Even though they'd wound up making love the next morning, he still felt spurned, and while sex was only one of the things he'd loved sharing with Annie, so much cascaded down from that. He guessed this was true with most couples; lovemaking — the experience of how they were together when emotions and feelings were that intense — was the thing that defined them as a unit. If it were absent or if it happened with anything less than real dedication, the rest of the relationship felt emptier. That was what had thrown him so badly that morning at the River's Turn: Annie had only seemed partially there, ultimately leading Maxwell to check out as well. It was as though their bodies continued to go through the motions while their souls had already left the building.

Maybe something like showing up unexpectedly in the middle of a workday could change the dynamic a bit. This is what guided Maxwell as he entered the neighborhood and what compelled him out of the car after he parked in the garage.

Joey was wearing a fireman's cap, toting a toy dinosaur, and wearing only a t-shirt and a training diaper when Maxwell entered. He was making roaring sounds — presumably his interpretation of how an allosaurus spoke

— and didn't seem to notice that his father had arrived right away. By the time Maxwell put his briefcase down, though, Joey had turned to him, screamed his name, and jumped into his arms.

It's definitely worth coming home early to get a reception like that, Maxwell thought as he carried his son into the living room. Annie wasn't there, so he called out for her. She didn't respond, so he called out again. This time, she called back that she was in the laundry room.

He headed off in that direction, still toting Joey in his arms. When he got to Annie, she was pulling dripping wet clothing from the washing machine.

"What are you doing home?" she said, looking at him for a half-second before pulling out a sodden shirt and dropping it in the laundry basket.

"I got a free pass for the afternoon. What's going on here?"

Annie pulled out a pair of underwear and threw it in the basket, the spray from it reaching his pant leg. "I'm doing laundry — and I'm having a great time with it. Isn't that obvious?"

"Doesn't the clothing usually come out less drenched than this?"

"It does if the freaking washing machine doesn't stop dead in the middle of a cycle."

"The washing machine is broken?"

Annie looked at him like he'd just soiled himself. "What gave you that idea?"

Joey took that moment to start roaring again and then hit Maxwell repeatedly on the head with the dinosaur. Maxwell thought it would be best to extricate Joey from this scene — not to mention that getting hit by the dinosaur hurt — so he said to Annie, "Give me a second to change," and took the boy into the bedroom so he could get out of his suit and into jeans.

Two minutes later, he had his son in front of the TV and he was back in the laundry room with his wife, who was still pulling out clothes and cursing the appliance that was putting her through such turmoil.

"So what happened here?" he said.

Annie threw a handful of clothing into the basket and then wiped her hands on the legs of her jeans. "Nothing that doesn't happen around here every single day."

"The washing machine breaks down every single day?"

Annie's eyes narrowed. "The washing machine breaks down, or the cable goes out during your son's favorite show, or the computer crashes, or Joey crashes...yeah, just about every day."

Maxwell was having a difficult time matching Annie's tone with the litany of household calamities. She was talking about minor mishaps as though the kitchen ceiling was caving in daily. "Why don't you go sit down and let me take care of this?"

"What do you know about repairing a washing machine?"

"I don't know anything about repairing a washing machine. Were you planning on fixing this yourself?"

She put a hand on her hip. "Don't be a smart-ass. I was going to call a repairman as soon as I got all of the clothes out."

Maxwell held up his hands in an attempt to calm Annie down. "I'll call a repairman. I'll get someone from Statewide to come down."

"Oh, right, I forgot; the *mayor* can call in a favor whenever he wants."

Maxwell was beginning to wonder if there'd been a short in the washing machine and if Annie had somehow been electrocuted. It was otherwise difficult to understand why she was reacting the way she was. "There's really no favor required. The people at Statewide are very good, and I see them regularly at Chamber meetings."

"Do whatever you want." Annie took several steps past him out of the laundry room and then turned back. "What are you doing here, anyway?"

"Some meetings got cancelled. I thought I'd take the opportunity to come home early."

"Why?"

Maxwell was beginning to ask himself the same question. "I thought the three of us could do something together."

Annie looked past him. For a moment, her expression grew contemplative, then seemingly confused. Then she darkened again. "It's good that you're home. This day has been a bear for me. I need to get out for a while."

Though his mood had dimmed, Maxwell was still willing to rally. "Great; let's go do something."

Again, Annie looked at him with eyes that didn't remind him in any way of their wedding day. "I didn't mean that I needed to get out with *all of us*. Joey's been a huge handful today. You take over. I'm going out for some fresh air."

Annie didn't stay around to discuss it. As was happening with increasing regularity, she took off immediately after announcing her intention to do so. Maxwell hadn't even gotten to the phone to call the repair people when he heard Annie's car start.

Joey was playing quietly with his dinosaur, no longer roaring, when Maxwell finished with Statewide a few minutes later. He got a stuffed monkey from the toy chest and sat down on the floor with his son to play-act for a while. A short while later, he buckled his son in his car seat and they headed off for ice cream.

It wasn't what he'd imagined for the afternoon, but these freebies didn't come along often. He would take advantage of it, and he would enjoy some bonus time with Joey. And at least the kid seemed to want to be with him.

∿

Annie got back after ten that night and went directly to bed. The next night, though, she was sitting on the couch after Maxwell finished getting Joey down for the night. She had her tablet in her hands, but she wasn't reading from it. Instead, she looked at him tentatively, as though she knew that they needed to discuss what had happened. That was unusual these days.

Often, Maxwell would begin such a conversation gradually, but that didn't seem to be the right thing to do here, especially since Annie seemed to be anticipating it. "What would you have done if I hadn't come home early yesterday?" he said.

Annie seemed confused by the question, obviously expecting him to come at this from a different angle. "What do you mean?"

"You seemed furious when I walked in. What were you going to do? Were you going to take a hatchet to the washing machine?"

Annie's brow wrinkled. "I'm furious a lot during the day; you're just not usually around to see it. The appliances generally survive."

"Why are you furious a lot, Annie? I understand getting pissed off when something breaks, but if you're furious *a lot* and the house is in fairly good shape, something else needs to be driving this."

Annie slumped back on the couch and her expression darkened. "Are you seriously asking me that question?"

Maxwell was asking the question seriously, but he wasn't asking it with the naivety that Annie seemed to be suggesting. He knew that Annie was frustrated. What he couldn't seem to do was get her to discuss it with him in a productive way. Maybe asking the obvious was a method for doing so, even if it made him seem more clueless than he was.

"What's making you furious, Annie?"

She shook her head slowly. "If you don't know, I have no interest in talking with you about it."

So much for that approach. "I don't have my head in the clouds. I know that you feel tied down by Joey. I know you wish you could get out more without dragging him around everywhere. So let's get started on fixing that. Do you think you'd like to work outside of the house again?"

Annie shrugged. "That's not really relevant, is it?"

"Of course it's relevant. You haven't been out of the workforce that long and the job market is stronger than it has been in years."

She spoke quietly and stiffly. "That wasn't what I was saying."

"Then what were you saying?"

Annie closed her eyes and then opened them slowly. "Our situation makes my getting a job very difficult."

It dawned on Maxwell that he had been standing during this conversation. He moved to sit on the other end of the couch. "I don't understand what you mean by that. Joey hasn't been great with babysitters, but that's because he's hardly had any practice. He'll adjust. And if you really want to do this, I'll help with the transition. I can steal some time if we plan ahead enough."

"Steal some time? Who are you stealing it from? Certainly not the people of Oldham."

Maxwell shifted a bit more in his wife's direction. "Annie, I'm running for mayor of a small New England city, not Tokyo. Do you really think it would be impossible for me to do this and spend a couple of mornings with my son? Hey, if I announce it now, it might even get me some votes."

Maxwell regretted saying that the second the words left his mouth.

Annie had of course picked up on this and she responded sharply. "So you're trying to help me out because it would benefit your campaign?"

"You know that isn't what I'm saying and I'm not suggesting this for that reason. I want you to be less furious. I want you to feel less trapped. This is about our family, nothing else."

Annie let that hang in the air for several seconds. Maxwell was about to say something to reinforce the point when she finally spoke.

"I might have bought that at some point, but that was before you made the unilateral decision to run for mayor. Really, Maxwell, how would this work? I go out and get a job and we hire a babysitter. I, of course, have to find the babysitter, because I'm the one who's creating the need for a babysitter. Joey has a tough time with separation a bunch of mornings, so you agree to go in late once or twice a week to help with the transition. It turns out that a couple of hours aren't anywhere near enough because Joey *hates* the babysitter. What happens then? Do you take more hours off? No, of course not. A couple of late starts to the day and the public thinks you're a great dad. More than that and they think you aren't taking this mayor thing seriously. What happens is that it becomes my responsibility to deal with it."

From the way Annie had delivered that speech, Maxwell got the impression that she'd rehearsed it in her head a few times during one of her furious days.

"That's an unnecessarily bleak perspective," he said.

She shook her head. "It's an entirely realistic perspective. Maybe now you can understand why I don't even want to think about getting a job. Just sounds like more heartache for me."

Maxwell was momentarily speechless. Annie had completely neutralized any attempt he was making to get them to a new place. She had already thought about going back to work; of course she had. She might have even thought about how doing so would give her the kind of new approach to the day that would return some equilibrium. Instead of suggesting this to Maxwell or at least engaging in a conversation about it when he broached it, though, she chose to see only the hurdles and the worst-case scenarios.

"So you're just going to hold on to your fury," he said, finding it impossible to keep the sense of accusation from his voice.

Annie looked off in the distance. "My fury and I have gotten very close. It keeps me good company."

That might have been the most honest thing Annie had said during the course of this conversation.

"Fury is destructive, Annie."

She looked him in the eyes for the first time. "Making decisions in a marriage when your spouse clearly opposes that decision is also destructive, Maxwell. You should have known that."

They were back to where they'd begun. When had his wife become so determined to maintain a narrative when he was trying to evolve it? They'd encountered snags before, places where their different interests knotted, and they'd always been able to untangle them. Why couldn't that happen now?

Annie stood and began to walk toward the bedroom.

"You don't have to worry about the appliances," she said. "I won't take a hatchet to them."

Chapter 7

~

Maxwell had never been particularly interested in the media spotlight. When he was working in Manhattan, he'd done a couple of spots on Bloomberg Radio and he'd once appeared on CNBC. In the years since he became president of the Chamber of Commerce, he'd do the occasional interview on local radio or cable news. None of it held very much meaning for him, though. It wasn't as though he'd contact everyone he knew to tell them to tune in or that he'd prepare for such appearances days in advance. He thought he was moderately mediagenic and if the media came looking for him, he was fine with making appearances. Never, though, did he seek them out.

That would need to change if he became mayor, however. Bruce did a weekly segment on a local radio station and fielded calls from both broadcast and print outlets throughout the region. In addition, Bruce regularly tracked down the media to promote something on his agenda. His aggressiveness in doing so was one of the many things that irked Mike Mills. Being in the news was part of the job — even if you didn't have the job yet. Over the course of the campaign, Maxwell had logged nearly as many media appearances as he had his entire life up to this point. It still felt a bit intrusive to him, but he was at least beginning to get accustomed to it.

Whether he was getting accustomed to it quickly enough to spar publicly with Mayor Bruce was something he would discover in the near future. During the mayor's radio segment last week, he invited Maxwell to share this week's interview time with him. Maxwell had no choice but to accept, though he knew he was entering the lion's den. The interviewer for the weekly segment, Tim Commerford, was known to toss the mayor softballs and had a long history of support for the incumbent. Maxwell entered the studio warily, seeing his job here as being much less about winning new voters than it was about avoiding losing those he already had.

The first twenty minutes of the half-hour segment nearly put Maxwell at ease. Commerford was no tougher on him than he was on the mayor, allowing Maxwell the opportunity to talk about his plans for economic growth, jobs building, and education. It was as though the radio host acknowledged the possibility of Maxwell's election and wanted to make sure he could keep the segment running with a new man in office. For his part, Mayor Bruce dealt with Maxwell respectfully, allowing Maxwell to make his points and avoiding the contentious behavior he'd exhibited during their first debate.

That was true until it was no longer true.

The mayor's attack was so swift and so unexpected that Maxwell felt as though he'd been pierced by a samurai's finest blade. "I admire some of my opponent's platform," Bruce said. "I only wish I could consider it without wondering about the motives behind it."

Maxwell's eyes widened. Meanwhile, Commerford's face brightened, clearly responding to the scent of controversy. "I'm not certain that I know what you mean by that, Mr. Mayor. Could you explain for our listeners?"

"Well, for example, Mr. Gold is talking about an aggressive initiative to bring new businesses to Oldham. That's an intriguing idea and one that I've certainly pursued from time to time during my tenure as mayor. Of course, what Mr. Gold isn't mentioning and is clearly hoping the people of our city won't think about on their own is that established businesses rarely uproot themselves or expand to other locations without an extremely good reason. And what I've learned as mayor is that those extremely good reasons often skirt legality in ways that those of us in the public trust are forbidden to pursue."

Maxwell could hardly believe what he was hearing. Was the mayor truly suggesting that Maxwell had been buying favors — while at the same time suggesting that the mayor himself had steered clear of anything that had to do with the commerce of influence?

"Mr. Mayor," Maxwell said, "I'm not sure that's a fair assessment of how businesses choose to relocate, especially the types of businesses I've suggested recruiting. Oldham is an extremely attractive market, especially for the culinary, artisan, and luxury sectors, and increasingly so in the tech sector. Those sectors don't need any reason other than the potential to grow their own businesses. Beyond this, my plan doesn't prioritize seeking businesses to leave their current locations for Oldham; the primary focus is on getting these businesses to open additional locations in Oldham. As you know, I've already had some success with this."

The mayor tipped his head forward as though he were thanking Maxwell for playing directly into his hand. "Yes, your success has been noted by my office. In fact, the legal department is examining it very carefully right now."

Maxwell's eyes nearly popped out of his head this time. "The legal department? Are you trying to suggest that there were improprieties in this deal?"

The mayor chose to look at Commerford rather than Maxwell. "It would be inappropriate for me to betray the details of any investigation on Tim's show, now, wouldn't it, Tim?"

Commerford chuckled. "I'm sorry to say that's true, Mr. Mayor, much as it would make great radio if it weren't."

"Hold on," Maxwell said. "I want to make sure I'm hearing you correctly. You're saying that the city has begun a legal investigation into the way we recruited Sabores to open their second location in Oldham?"

"Mr. Gold, we're in a public forum. I've already told you that I can't give you any further information while the microphones are turned on."

Maxwell stared at the mayor for what amounted to ten seconds of dead air. Finally, he attempted to gather himself. "Investigate anything you want. I have nothing to hide, nor does anyone on my staff. We recruited Sabores the same way we will recruit all new businesses to our town: by showing them how we are the ideal market for their expansion. There's nothing even remotely illegal about that."

The mayor offered the kind of thin laugh that was more befitting a backwoods tyrant than the head of a cosmopolitan Connecticut River Valley community. "That may very well be true, Mr. Gold. I suppose it's too soon to say." He turned to Commerford. "Tim, don't you have any other questions?"

Commerford switched topics and the interview ended only a few minutes later. Maxwell felt winded, as though he'd been doing the entire segment while running uphill. As the host went to commercial and said goodbye to his guests, Maxwell turned on the mayor.

"If you have any suspicions of illegal conduct, I have a right to know what you're accusing me of," he said heatedly.

Bruce offered another thin laugh and then spoke calmly. "I didn't say we were accusing you of anything, Maxwell."

Maxwell folded his arms in front of him. "You only said that your legal department was examining the deal carefully."

The mayor gave a barely perceptible nod. "Of course they are. Our legal department examines every deal carefully. That's their job."

"So you're not saying that you think I did anything illegal in recruiting Sabores."

Bruce delivered an exaggerated shrug. "I have no reason to suspect that you did.

Besides, I didn't need to say anything of the sort — you did it for me."

With that, the mayor handed his notepad to his assistant and left the studio.

Mike, who'd been with Maxwell in the studio the entire time, clapped him on the shoulder. It was probably a gesture of support, but it felt like a pounding.

Maxwell shook his head and turned to his campaign manager. "He played me."

"Like a virtuoso."

Maxwell took a deep breath and exhaled slowly. "I suck at this."

"Let's not draw conclusions based on insufficient data."

Maxwell laughed thinly. "Which is your way of saying that you also think I suck at this."

Mike held Maxwell's eyes for a long moment. "Let's not do any events with the mayor again until we've done some additional prep."

If Mike had said, "Yes, you suck at this," it would have hurt less. Maxwell groaned and exited the studio with Mike. He felt like a middle-schooler trying to play one-on-one with an NBA point guard.

The gap between himself and his opponent had never seemed wider.

∽

Two nights later, Maxwell was still stinging from the way the mayor had shown him up. Some of his staff had tried to spin it as something that would ultimately hurt Bruce with voters because he came off as mean and manipulative, but Mike didn't attempt to gloss over it at all. Maxwell appreciated Mike's candor, but it made it harder to put his flub behind him.

The first thing that helped Maxwell avoid thinking about the bombed interview all the time was his evening play date with Joey. Unlike some others recently, this one was not due to a sudden departure by his wife. This one had actually been on the books for months. A couple of Annie's college friends were in the area from Chicago and they'd gotten together for dinner out. Annie had seemed a little more relaxed tonight in anticipation of the dinner, and she was neither clipped nor put-upon when she spoke to him. Maybe this was something they should plan more often; giving her a regular night out alone might actually do more for their marriage than planning a regular night out together.

Maxwell made his son and himself peanut butter and jelly sandwiches for dinner. He was actually capable of preparing two or three nutritious meals, and if this became more of a regular thing, he knew he'd have to do so when dinner was his responsibility, but PB&J seemed to better fit the tone of this particular evening. Maxwell did put out some baby carrots as well, so at least a few of the food groups were represented.

After dinner, Maxwell and Joey played a spirited game of Nerf soccer in the living room. Joey was still capable of walking into walls on his way in and out of a room, but his coordination was definitely improving and he was beginning to do a good job of dribbling with the ball. Maybe by this time next year, they'd be thinking about signing him up for a recreational league soccer team. Joey's goal was the double-wide doorway leading into the foyer while Maxwell's was the space under the coffee table, which would have required Jedi-like precision to shoot into. This helped make the game competitive, as Maxwell didn't need to try hard to miss. Still, Joey got the best of his father in this contest, winning 8-0 before wandering over to the toy chest in mid-dribble to pull out his SpongeBob and Patrick action figures. He still had the soccer ball with him, and he kicked it aside, moved toward the middle of the room, and sat on the floor. Picking up on the clue that the game was over, Maxwell joined him there.

Joey was doing something with Sponge-Bob that Maxwell couldn't discern. He appeared to be grooming him, the way a gorilla might, though it was probably something else entirely. Maxwell picked up Patrick and started talking in his approximation of the sea star's TV voice.

"Hey, SpongeBob, what are we going to do today," Patrick said.

Joey grinned at him (or more specifically Patrick), but didn't say anything, choosing instead to get his Batmobile from next to the toy chest and put SpongeBob in it. Maxwell wasn't positive that Patrick was being invited along for a ride, but they *were* best friends, so Maxwell just assumed so and put Patrick in the passenger seat. Joey then drove them out of the living room, down the hall, and into his bedroom, where he took SpongeBob out of the car and put him on top of his bed. After doing this, Joey looked at Patrick, then up at his father, and then back down at Patrick again. Maxwell interpreted this to mean that he was supposed to put the sea star on the bed as well.

"Is it night-night time for SpongeBob and Patrick?" Maxwell said.

Joey shook his head as though this were the most absurd question he'd ever heard. He then picked up SpongeBob and started bouncing him on the bed, as Joey himself had done many, many times. Identifying his cue, Maxwell did the same with Patrick, never bouncing as high, because he figured sponges were springier than sea stars. For perhaps two minutes, they did nothing other than bounce the dolls. Joey probably could have continued to do so for another twenty minutes, but Maxwell's attention span wasn't nearly as long. He had Patrick do a seat-drop, then a somersault, then a belly-flop. Joey obviously found this inspiring, because he started having SpongeBob do all sorts of acrobatics, including bouncing from his feet on the mattress to his head on the pillow and then back to his feet. Maxwell hoped that Joey wasn't planning a similar trick the next time he himself used his bed as a trampoline. Joey laughed hard while he was doing this, which caused Maxwell to laugh and invent even more ridiculous stunts for Patrick to perform. To an outsider, they might have seemed manic, maybe even a bit unhinged, but Maxwell was loving this because his son seemed to be loving it.

Then, in typical unceremonious fashion, Joey stopped suddenly, sat SpongeBob on the bed, and turned to his father.

"Where's Mom and Dad?" Joey said.

Maxwell sat Patrick on the bed next to SpongeBob, the two best friends not quite touching. "Well, Mom is out tonight with some friends. We talked about this. But Dad's right here, Joe."

Joey regarded his father with disapproving eyes and then picked up his action figure. "Where's SpongeBob mom and dad?"

Maxwell understood this to mean that Joey wanted to know about SpongeBob's mother and father. That made more sense. The two of them had watched dozens of episodes of the cartoon show, but Maxwell couldn't remember any reference to Sponge-Bob's parents.

"You know, I think SpongeBob is a grownup, so he doesn't live with his mom and dad anymore."

"No."

That wasn't right? What part? Was Joey saying that SpongeBob wasn't a grownup — he had a job and his own house — or was he saying that he thought that SpongeBob still lived with his mother and father. "Where do you think they are?"

Joey stared at the doll for nearly a minute, as though trying to divine some truth from it. "I don't know. That's why I ask you."

That was the most complex thought Joey had ever expressed to Maxwell, and Maxwell wanted to honor it by giving the boy a considered answer. "I have a feeling that they live in a different town. Maybe they live in the town *next to* Bikini Bottom. SpongeBob goes to visit them all the time and his mom makes lasagna for him. For some reason we never get to see that in the cartoon, though."

"No. Not right."

Maxwell wondered if he'd blown it with the lasagna. Should he have said something that Joey was more familiar with like grilled chicken...or PB&Js? "You know what, Joe? Maybe that's not right. Maybe they live next door. Maybe they have dinner together at the Krusty Krab three times a week."

"No!"

Joey picked up his action figure now and extended it toward Maxwell. "Where's Mom and Dad?"

Maxwell really just wanted to go back to bouncing the dolls on the bed, but that was probably a distant memory for his son at this point. What was Joey looking for?

"Oh, I remember now, Joe. SpongeBob's mom and dad live in the pineapple house with him, but they have really big jobs so they aren't home that much. That's why we don't see them in the cartoons. But they really love SpongeBob."

"Nooooooooooooo!"

Joey threw his action figure against the wall and then threw himself on his carpet, crying. Playtime was definitely over. Now it was time for Maxwell to manage his son. Hopefully, he'd be able to do so before Annie got home.

Chapter 8

~

Maxwell met Mike for breakfast the next morning. Before Maxwell left for the diner, Joey asked him to bounce Sponge-Bob and Patrick on the bed with him for a few minutes, showing no hangover from the previous night. Maxwell wished he could be even a quarter as resilient as his son, though he also wished he had even the remotest clue why his son's emotional state seemed so fragile. This had been going on long enough by this point to be well past a phase. If it continued much longer, they were going to have to take him to see someone.

Mike was already seated and had likely been there for a while. Multiple sections of the newspaper were strewn about the table, and Mike was holding his coffee cup out to the waitress for a refill. As Maxwell slid into the booth across from Mike, Mike threw the papers on the bench next to him and rearranged himself. His eyes were active, as though the refill he'd just gotten was far from his first.

"We're gonna hit Bruce where he lives," Mike said, sounding like a high school football coach.

"I have no idea what you mean by that."

"We're going into the belly of the beast."

Maxwell put his napkin in his lap. "Is this National Cliché Day? If I'd known, I would have, um, come *loaded for bear*."

Mike smiled at him. "Now you're getting into the spirit."

Maxwell shook his head briskly. "Do you think we can press rewind here? Good morning, Mike. Did you have a nice evening?"

Mike seemed to realize that he was coming across as overly amped. He sat back, took a deep breath, let it out, and then took a sip from his coffee cup (which probably defeated the purpose of the rest of the exercise). "Good morning, Maxwell. Yes, I had a good night last night. Is everyone in the family well?"

"Fine, thanks."

"Can we get to work now?"

Maxwell laughed. No one would ever describe him as unambitious, but next to his campaign manager, he probably seemed like a slacker. "As soon as I order breakfast."

"I already ordered for us."

"You ordered breakfast for *me*?"

"You order the same thing every time we come here — two eggs over easy, ham, hash browns, and wheat toast. I took the calculated risk of assuming that you weren't going to head into uncharted territory today."

"That was a bold move."

"*Were* you going to head into uncharted territory?"

"Of course not; I always order the same thing."

Mike offered him a half-smile. "Can we get down to business now?"

"Sure."

Mike moved forward again. "You're ready to take the gloves off, right?"

"We seem to have gone back to vague clichés."

Mike's eyes flitted momentarily, which Maxwell knew was his way of recalculating. "I assume you're as furious as I am about the way Bruce treated you during the interview the other day."

The waitress came with coffee for Maxwell — coffee he didn't order, but would have — and Maxwell added some half and half before taking a sip. "Yeah, of course I am."

"The staff is apoplectic. I swear Steve was only three short of the world record for obscenities used in a two-minute period. Meanwhile I think Alecia — she's remarkable, by the way — somehow managed to take it more personally than you did."

Maxwell found this surprisingly charming. He knew Steve was on his side, but this suggested a level of emotional involvement that Maxwell hadn't ascribed to the man. He wasn't surprised that Alecia had reacted the way she had. For one, he'd seen her reaction himself the last time they spoke, and for another, he'd been becoming increasingly aware that she was more heavily invested in the campaign than made sense on the surface.

"I should probably discuss it with the staff," he said. "They need to know that I understand that I had some responsibility in this."

Mike put up a hand. "Don't be ridiculous. I'm sure most of them know at some level that you got caught off guard. But right now, they see the mayor as Golem. That's a good thing. Especially given what we're going to do next."

"And what exactly is that?"

Mike pulled out his iPad, accessed a document, and handed the tablet to Maxwell. "Here's all the documentation on the new jobs-for-favors scandal. We have multiple sources for everything. There's no way Bruce can deny this one."

Maxwell looked through some of the documentation, including transcripts of statements from witnesses. Bruce had been the object of many claims of corruption over the course of his tenure, but rarely was there as much to back up the claims as there seemed to be here. "The mayor is a hell of a Boy Scout, isn't he?"

"A model citizen. So here's how I see us capitalizing on this: we leak this to one of the bigger political sites. Alecia can help us out with that because she seems to know everyone. They'll shrug, but they'll probably run with it because they need a constant flow of content, and ugly is always good for them. As soon as that hits, we release a statement to all the local media. Then we flood social media with indignation over Bruce's actions. And then we get you on TV and radio talking about it. Dream scenario? We guilt Tim Commerford into having you back on his show to express your disappointment over the mayor's breach of the public trust."

Maxwell was a little dazed from the torrent coming from his campaign manager. "You have a whole action plan lined up, don't you?"

Mike took back the tablet. "I literally have a whole action plan. It's in a different file. Do you want me to call it up for you?"

At that point, their food arrived, which allowed for a much-needed break. Maxwell added some hot sauce to his eggs while Mike folded brown sugar into his oatmeal.

For maybe a minute, neither man spoke, but Maxwell was contending with his internal dialogue. Mike had certainly dug up a tremendous amount of evidence to support his allegations. It might even be enough to allow the state to initiate some kind of legal action against the mayor. While Maxwell was convinced that most Oldham residents tended to ignore Bruce's indiscretions, he was fairly certain he could shift some voters to his side with the release of this information.

Even if this could help him win, though, did he want to win this way? He recalled the conversation with Alecia after Mike first broke the news to the team. For *you, not against him — that's what we're going for.*

"This is awfully negative stuff, Mike."

Mike swallowed a spoonful of oatmeal and took another sip of coffee. "What Bruce did to you on the radio was negative. This is just educating the voter."

"We've been saying all along that we weren't going to sling mud."

Mike put down his spoon and focused his attention completely on Maxwell. "We weren't anticipating something like this, though we certainly should have. We have always wanted to take the high road, but I don't see how this contradicts that. We're not making this up; Bruce very definitely did all of this."

"Still, I…"

"And more to the point, we need it. We can't kid ourselves about the numbers, Maxwell. They weren't comforting *before* the radio interview. They're not likely to be better now."

Mike had rarely been that blunt with him and Maxwell found it a bit jarring. Mike wasn't saying anything Maxwell didn't already know. He was more than aware of the numbers and equally aware that those numbers probably took a hit after the interview. However, hearing it aloud made the reality of it harsher, made it more real.

At the same time, though, this was where one's response to tests mattered. Anyone could maintain his integrity when it could be done without consequences. It was something else entirely when you did so even if it could cost you.

"I don't want to be that guy, Mike."

Mike looked at him with an expression that made it clear that he truly didn't understand Maxwell's thinking. "What guy? The next mayor of Oldham?"

"I don't want to be the guy who becomes the next mayor of Oldham by sucker-punching the current mayor of Oldham."

"You can actually say that after what he did to you the other day?"

"Yes, even after that. The idea is to make the people of this town want me, not to have them take me because they dislike me less than the other guy."

Mike gestured to the waitress for more coffee. The waitress refilled Maxwell's nearly-full cup at the same time. "The idea is to get into office. Whether or not the people of Oldham adore you on Election Day is irrelevant. We both know they'll adore you once you're mayor."

Maxwell took a bite of his eggs and then a sip of his coffee, avoiding eye contact with his campaign manager while he did so. He took another sip of coffee, put down his mug, and then looked at Mike. "No action plan. Not *this* action plan, anyway. You want to use this as a way to rally the staff and spur them to come up with new ideas to make sure a corrupt mayor doesn't get another term? I'm all for that. But this news doesn't break from our camp, and if the news breaks elsewhere, we refocus the media and the voters on the issues, not on the scandal."

Mike scoffed. "Challengers rarely get opportunities this golden, Maxwell."

"I can appreciate that. This is the approach I want to take, though. Let's win this on our terms. Let's win this in a way that we can feel good about afterward."

Mike let out a little chuckle. "I just want to win it."

"So let's do that. But without the ugly stuff."

Mike played with his oatmeal, looking considerably less animated than he had ten minutes earlier. "You know that he wouldn't be nearly as generous to you, right?"

"Yet another thing we can feel good about after we beat him."

∿

A few nights later came one of the two fund-raisers Annie had agreed to attend. She'd signed on for this months ago after a long, occasionally strained conversation with Maxwell and Mike about the expectations from spouses during a campaign, which turned out to be the last long conversation the three of them would have up to this point. Now, given the increased chilliness between Annie and Maxwell — her night out hadn't provided the hinted thaw — he half expected her to find an excuse for backing out at the last minute. Just after Maxwell got home from work to change for the event, Joey slipped rounding a corner and got a rug burn on his right knee. Maxwell assumed that the crying that ensued would cause Annie to say that she couldn't leave her son alone with a babysitter after such a trauma, but she chose not to take the opportunity.

An hour into the event, though, Maxwell had begun to wish she had. Annie looked beautiful — she always looked beautiful — in a black dress cut just above the knee. She'd always loved dressing up and she'd taken extreme care in doing so tonight. When they got to the catering hall, she started socializing instantly, toting her Champagne glass from one donor to another during cocktails. Maxwell should have noticed that she was drinking that Champagne rather quickly, and that she seemed to have the wait staff on speed-dial for refills. Suggesting that she slow down might have led to a tense exchange, but that still would have been better than what he was facing now.

"Oh, you should see him with Joey," Annie was saying to an attractive forty-something woman and the slightly older man standing next to her. Maxwell couldn't place either of them, but if they were in this room, they'd either paid handsomely or had already donated a considerable amount to the campaign. "He's a great playmate for our son. But, really, Maxwell has always done his best work on all fours."

Annie was speaking loudly enough for Maxwell to hear her clearly, even though he was twenty feet away and flanked by several executives from Content Algorithm, a media firm that had moved to Oldham less than two years earlier. Maxwell considered it something of a coup to get them to this event, since he'd been certain that Mayor Bruce had offered them significant considerations to convince them to bring their offices here. Maxwell found most conversation at events such as these to be banal, but he'd been in a fascinating talk with the CA people, getting a better sense of how they used their data mining techniques to find genuinely interested customers for their clients. When Annie's words made their way to him, though, his attention shot in that direction.

"And he *does* try to show up for dinner once or twice a week, which I suppose is better than a lot of guys in his position. He's passed out on the couch an hour later, but a girl can't have everything now, can she? And he is a man on a mission."

Maxwell wasn't certain if Annie's voice was getting louder or if he was just more attuned to it, but it seemed as though she was speaking with enough volume to get the attention of everyone in the room. Certainly, she'd gotten the attention of the CA people.

"We haven't had the chance to meet your wife yet," said Michael Rother, CA's Chief Technology Officer.

Now that he no longer needed to pretend to be listening to every word his group was saying, Maxwell glanced over at Annie. She looked radiant, but Maxwell could identify her drunk posture, the one where she listed slightly to the left and turned her right foot inward. It was a sign that she needed to sit, though she didn't seem to be looking for a place to rest.

Maxwell turned back to Michael. "I'd love to introduce you. There's such a crowd here, though. Maybe we can set up a dinner sometime soon."

Michael nodded knowingly. It was very clear that he understood what was going on. What wasn't clear was whether this was going to affect CA's support for his campaign.

"That would be great, Maxwell. You know, I'm a pretty good student of body language, and I think your wife is desperate to be rescued from those people she's talking to."

Maxwell knew a fair amount about body language himself and he knew that Annie was signaling no such thing. Michael was clearly giving him an out.

"Thanks for picking up on that. I'd better go save her, huh?"

He headed toward Annie, needing to say hello to a couple of people on his way there.

"I guess it really comes down to the choice between love and success," Annie was now saying as Maxwell approached. He was relatively certain she couldn't see him coming, though he wasn't at all sure that would have mattered. "Ice cream sundaes with the family or fancy parties."

As he got closer, Maxwell could see that several groups of people were watching Annie now. A number of them offered Maxwell understanding smiles, which meant two things: they sympathized with his situation and they were going to be watching how he handled it.

Annie had never gone off like this in public before. For the most part, she simply stayed silent at events, smiling on occasion and offering the briefest possible answers when questioned. She was breaking with the script tonight — in so many ways. Maxwell needed to get her out of this situation, but doing so was going to be a delicate task.

He approached Annie from her left side, the side that wasn't holding the Champagne glass that had been recently refilled for maybe the dozenth time. Maxwell was beginning to suspect that the waiter worked for the Bruce campaign. When he got next to her, he put an arm around her shoulders and kissed her temple. He pulled her closer to him for a moment and then let go to shake the hands of the people she was with. It was at that point that he saw Mike coming from across the room. At a forty-five degree angle, Maxwell saw his sister Corrina approaching as well.

"I hate to steal Annie from you," Maxwell said to the two donors, "but we have this thing we need to do before dinner."

Annie spoke before the donors could react in any way. "We have a thing?"

Maxwell turned toward his wife. "That media thing."

Annie's voice grew again in volume. "We have a media thing? You know how much I hate the media."

Mike had moved to just outside of their circle at this point. "Oh, come on, Annie. *I'm* a member of the media."

Annie's posture stiffened. "What's your point, Mike?"

Maxwell took Annie's elbow. "Well, obligations are obligations, I'm afraid. We've got to go to a little meeting room just outside of the ballroom."

Annie grimaced, but she let Maxwell lead her out, with Mike and Corrina following. As they got close to the door, Annie said to him, "You didn't tell me anything about a media thing. I didn't *agree* to a media thing."

Maxwell managed to get her out of the ballroom before responding. "There isn't any media thing, Annie."

She turned to see her sister-in-law and Maxwell's campaign manager and she glared at both of them. "Then what the hell are we doing out here?"

"I'm taking you out of the situation."

She pivoted back to him, doing so fast enough that she teetered a bit in the process, causing Maxwell to wonder if she'd had even more Champagne than he'd estimated. "You're taking me out of the situation? Are you giving me a *time out*?"

Corrina chose that moment to step in. "You were a little loud in there, Annie."

"Nobody asked you!" Annie said sharply.

Thankfully, Mike was smart enough to stay out of the fray, though his presence alone made this more complicated. Maxwell touched his wife's arm softly. "There are a lot of people I need to have on my side in there. I really don't need them hearing that I'm a lousy husband, especially when half the stuff you're saying isn't even true."

Annie seemed confused for a second and then her expression darkened. "Are you telling me you don't want me in there? You beg me to come to these ridiculous events and when I finally do, you kick me out?"

"You've made it clear that you really don't want to be here. And you're right that I have been begging you to come to these events. You do understand that I wasn't begging you to come so you could make me look awful in front of my supporters, right?"

"So you're kicking me out?"

"You've had an awful lot to drink. I think it might be best if you went home. I'll get a car for you."

"I can run her home," Corrina said.

Maxwell expected another outburst from Annie, but she chose to simmer rather than explode. She took a couple of steps toward Corrina and then turned back to him. "Let's just be clear about what happened tonight," she said.

Throughout their relationship, Maxwell had always tried to alleviate Annie's anger. He felt no inclination to do so now. "I'm very clear about what happened tonight."

Her face got as close to ugly as Maxwell imagined it was possible for it to get. "This isn't just going to go away."

"Believe me, Annie, I realize that."

For a moment, it appeared that she was going to say more. Instead, she turned toward Corrina and then walked past her toward the exit. Corrina offered a sympathetic glance before she reached into her purse for her car keys.

Maxwell shook his head slowly before turning to go back into the ballroom. Mike walked with him.

"I don't want to discuss this," Maxwell said.

Mike simply threw up his hands in surrender.

"Frosty" didn't begin to define the interactions between Maxwell and Annie over the next few days. She was already in bed when Maxwell got home from the fundraiser and didn't even bother to pretend to be asleep when he got in next to her. Instead, she moved to the far edge of the bed, facing away from him. Maxwell guessed that if she'd had time to install a moat between them she would have.

Dinner the next night was more of the same, with Annie making it clear that she was actively not speaking to Maxwell. She engaged Joey in conversation much more than usual, and if Maxwell attempted to participate, she would stare at him for a moment and then go back to her son. For his part, Maxwell wasn't willing to make any conciliatory gestures, any attempt to break the tension between them. What Annie had done was egregious, and while he was sure that alcohol contributed to the severity of it, he was equally certain that it was, to some degree, calculated. She'd known what she was doing and how it was likely to be interpreted. She might have even planned it before she arrived at the ballroom. If he really wanted to get paranoid, Maxwell could convince himself that she'd planned it from the moment she agreed to attend the event, which was

141

a much more likely explanation for her being there than that she'd been willing to offer token support to his campaign. Fortunately, the episode didn't seem to get any play in the media, though it was difficult to gauge the effect of any whispering that went on among attendees. Alecia had been listing carefully to social media in an effort to identify any such effect.

Now it was Saturday morning and Annie was of course again out of the house. Maxwell had gotten up early with Joey (it was his day, though it increasingly seemed to be his responsibility to take care of Joey any day he didn't go into work), and they were eating breakfast in the kitchen when Annie entered, kissed Joey on the top of the head, and grabbed her car keys from the counter. Maxwell didn't exchange any words with his wife, but he watched her angrily as she left. Maxwell must have still had most of that anger on his face when he looked at Joey again, because the boy's expression changed instantly when they made eye contact, and he got down from his chair and left the room less than a minute later. There was a lesson there that Maxwell made sure to learn.

A few minutes later, Maxwell went to check on his son, but when he saw the boy playing quietly with one of his action figures, he decided that everything was okay and that he should leave him alone. He went back into the kitchen to clean up their dishes and then sat at the table with a coffee refill and the *New York Times*.

Several minutes after that, Joey came bounding into the room. Maxwell looked up at him and Joey held his gaze for a couple of seconds. Then the boy ran up to the table, climbed up on a chair — and swept the ceramic bowl in the middle of the table onto the floor. The bowl, a Christmas present from Maxwell to Annie from a local artist, atomized on the floor, breaking into more pieces than Maxwell would have considered possible.

As soon as it happened, Joey ran out of the room. Maxwell was so stunned by the action that he couldn't move for maybe thirty seconds. Joey had certainly broken other items. Given how often he bounced off of things, it was fortunate that he'd never broken any bones. This was a deliberate act, though. Joey had come in here bent on destruction. Maybe it turned out to be the bowl because it was the first thing Joey saw, but Maxwell was certain that Joey had run into the kitchen with the intention of breaking something. That had never happened before.

Once he got past the initial shock, Maxwell went to find his son. Joey was standing in the middle of the den, poised to dash off, as though he'd been waiting for his father to arrive before racing away. Maxwell took a step toward him, and Joey ran right past him and down the hall. Maxwell followed him, telling himself not to tread too heavily as he did so. He didn't want the kid to envision him as a stalking, punitive giant. This was about trying to understand why his son had done what he did, not about exacting a toll for his having done so. Joey stopped by the hall bathroom and Maxwell stopped ten feet away from him. Was Joey going to try to close himself off in there? Did he know how to lock the door? If so, where was the key?

They stood in this pose for several long seconds. Finally, Maxwell said, "Joe, what happened in there?"

In response, Joey took off toward his room. Trying to keep calm, but finding it more and more difficult to do so, Maxwell again followed him. When he got into the room, though, he couldn't immediately find his son. He looked in the closet and behind the stand-up poster of Elmo before noticing that the boy had burrowed under his bed.

Maxwell sat on the floor near him. At this point, any anger he'd felt about Joey breaking the bowl had dissipated. However, he was still completely mystified. "Joey, why'd you do that? You know that the bowl was one of our special things."

Maxwell didn't expect him to be able to articulate a response. Their conversation about SpongeBob's parents the other night was the most nuanced discussion they'd ever had, and getting Joey to explain himself here would have required another level of conversational skill entirely. However, he did not anticipate what came next — a scream that might have shattered a window or two if it hadn't been muffled by the mattress. The scream went on for at least ten seconds before Joey paused for breath.

"Joey, I'm trying to understand –"

The screaming began again, with increased intensity and greater duration. Maxwell again waited it out.

"Joey, I'm not –"

Maxwell didn't get the chance to tell his son what he wasn't going to do before the howling restarted.

Maxwell had no idea how to handle this. This certainly wasn't the first time that Joey had done something that required a talking-to, but in the past, he had always been willing to sit on his lap and listen to any course correction his father might suggest. It was obvious now, though, that Joey was just going to start screaming as soon as Maxwell said anything. He might not even be willing to come out from under his bed until Maxwell left the room.

It really would be great if something *in my life was going well,* Maxwell thought. He sat there and waited. When Joey had stayed quiet for a few minutes, he reached under the bed, found his son's hand — thankfully, the boy didn't pull away — and gave it a little squeeze. Then he stood up and went into the kitchen to clean up the mess.

Chapter 9

~

The cold war between Maxwell and Annie continued for another week. Maxwell had never let a conflict with his wife go unaddressed for this long, and he found it illuminating to see that she hadn't made any effort in the absence of his doing so. Would this have always been the case? When they'd had troubles in the past, would she have just let the ill will fester indefinitely? Maxwell would never have thought this was possible — Annie was as invested in the health of their marriage as he, wasn't she? — but now he wasn't so sure.

Regardless, he found that he'd reached the point where he simply couldn't let it go on any longer. Yes, he was still angry with Annie over her actions at the fundraiser, but it was toxic to keep living with a cloud over their household. Between Annie's indifference and Joey's unpredictable behavior, Maxwell found his gut seizing a bit on his drives home. He'd never had that experience before, and it wasn't something he could allow himself to grow accustomed to.

So that Friday night, eight days after the fundraiser, Maxwell put Joey to bed and then went into the den to deal with the issue head-on. As was often the case, Annie's eyes were locked on a screen, in this case the television. As soon as he entered the room, though, she got up to leave, as she had several times in the past week.

"Don't go, Annie; we need to talk."

She actually took two additional steps out of the room before she stopped. "Why do we need to talk?"

Maxwell moved to sit on the couch, hoping she would do the same. "Are you comfortable with this?"

"With what?"

"With what's going on between us. Do you *like* acting as though I don't exist?"

"I know you exist, Maxwell."

"Yeah, I don't know what I was saying. You obviously know I exist because you might have accidentally bumped into me if you weren't so consciously trying to avoid me."

Annie scowled, which Maxwell actually considered to be a positive thing. At least she was reacting.

"You want to talk," she said.

"We need to talk."

"You really want to talk."

"I do, Annie."

"Okay, Maxwell, let's talk. Let's talk about how horribly you embarrassed me last week."

Maxwell offered a joyless laugh. "Are we doing a role-reversal thing here? Are you taking my role in this conversation?"

Annie did sit on the couch at that point, though as far on the other side of it as she possibly could. "Oh, give me a break. Don't try to make this out like you were the injured party here."

Maxwell's eyes widened. "I *was* the injured party. *You* were saying disparaging things about *me* at a public event. I think that qualifies as injury."

"At which point you shunted me out of the room and sent me away. You don't think anyone noticed that you'd banished me? You don't think that *injury* was worse?"

Maxwell was having a difficult time wrestling with Annie's logic here. Did she truly feel as though he'd made a spectacle of her at the fundraiser, or was she simply reaching for any weapon that might be in her arsenal?

"Yes, some people noticed you were gone," he said in measured tones. "A few of them asked me about it and I told them that you got a call from the babysitter while we were doing our 'interview.' Did you think I'd gone back into the ballroom and announced that I'd thrown my lunatic wife out of the party?"

Annie looked downward and shook her head slowly. "I'm not sure what you would have done."

Maxwell rolled his eyes. "You know me, Annie. Give me a little credit."

Annie seemed abashed by this comment. "I know you? I'm not sure that's the case, really. I *knew* you. I very definitely knew you. But the man I knew is very different from the man who is running for mayor."

This conversation was beginning to feel like the signage conversations during the Chamber meetings. "Different in what way?"

Annie took a couple of seconds to answer. "The man I knew always put me first."

Maxwell moved forward a bit on the couch. "I still put you first. You and Joey are the center of my life."

Annie sniffed at this. Was she dismissing the statement? Or was she unhappy with Maxwell's inclusion of their son?

"It's impossible for me to believe that you mean that," she said. "From the day you decided to become a candidate — something I emphatically asked you not to do — you have been focused exclusively on yourself. You've become this local celebrity with speeches and events and interviews while I'm the housewife in sweatpants making you dinner and taking care of our child."

That was hardly a fair depiction, but Maxwell decided to deal with this on Annie's terms. "I never asked you to play that role."

"What other role could I play? I refused to be your bauble standing next to you while you addressed your constituency, so this was the only option I had."

Forget about dealing with this on her terms. "There are so many things wrong with what you just said. For one thing, I never would have treated you as a 'bauble.' Mayor Bruce's wife is out there hosting her own functions and delivering her own speeches, and she's been doing so since his first term. You would have been great at that — you were always better at dealing with the public than me. But even if you didn't want to do that, it hardly meant that the only other choice was to stay locked up in the house with Joey velcroed to your side."

Annie didn't react other than to look away. Maxwell saw this as an opening, an indication that she wasn't going to strike back instantly with a recitation of her plight. That meant it was time for him to dial back his tone. If he wanted things to get better between them, he needed to soften the way he spoke now. Annie had never responded well

to him when he was angry, and it was time to
tamp down his anger so they could move on.

"Listen, Annie," he said softly, "I know
you didn't want me to do this. I'd hoped you
would understand why it was important for
me to do so, and I'd even hoped that you'd
come to enjoy it once we got going. I'm still
hoping for that. You really would be amazing
during a campaign. Whatever happens with
the election, though — and I really have no
idea what is going to happen — I want you
to know that I understand why you're feeling so frustrated. I'm going to make more
time for us. I know you think that won't be
possible, but I'm certain I can do it. And I'll
support anything you want to do with your
life. Sweatpants, business suits, I don't know,
a football uniform...whatever clothes you
want to wear, I'll do whatever I can to help
you wear them."

Annie looked downward again and didn't
say anything. Maxwell thought he might have
gotten through to her, at least a bit. From what
he could see of her face, it was obvious that she
was recalibrating as well. If they both moved
a bit closer to the middle, there was a good
chance they could pull together again. Maybe
the fundraiser was rock bottom and they were
ready to start climbing out.

Then Annie chuckled. It wasn't the kind of chuckle people made when they'd just thought of something funny.

"You really think we can just put everything behind us, don't you?" she said thinly.

Her tone actually chilled him. "We can find the right kind of compromise for our future. That's the important thing."

She chuckled again, and this time she looked up at him. Her eyes were stony. "So the past doesn't matter to you?"

Maxwell was feeling increasingly uneasy, even though he wasn't sure why he was suddenly so uncomfortable. Though he sometimes couldn't understand her actions — increasingly so these days — Maxwell could read his wife. And what he was reading now signaled danger. "Of course the past matters to me. I love most of our past and I'm completely willing to move on from this rough patch."

She turned sharply to face him, and it felt like a confrontation. "Let me tell you something about the past. The recent past. The past since you decided to ignore me and run for mayor. I'm guessing you're not going to *love* this. Do you remember Marty Balin?"

"Your high school boyfriend?" Maxwell said tentatively.

Annie's voice grew stronger. "Did you know he came to our twentieth reunion last year?"

Maxwell was becoming increasingly uneasy. "No, I didn't."

"Probably because you'd already started campaigning and you were too busy working the room. I didn't see much of you that night."

Maxwell didn't remember it the same way. In fact, he remembered trying to get Annie on the dance floor multiple times while she chose instead to catch up with old girlfriends. "So you saw Marty at the reunion?"

"And then again a few days later. And then a few days after that."

Maxwell felt pinpricks in his fingers. "What are you saying, Annie?"

Annie locked eyes with him. "I'm saying what you think I'm saying. I'm saying that the past and the present are pretty freaking intertwined and that the past has a pretty big impact on the future, too."

Maxwell no longer needed to wonder why he was feeling uncomfortable. "Are you having a thing with Marty? Is that where you've been going?"

Annie scoffed. "Marty was just passing through. He's down in Florida now, I believe."

That statement did nothing to alleviate the tension Maxwell was feeling. "But you *had* a thing with him."

"It was a moment, Maxwell. But here's the point: it was a great moment. It was the kind of moment you and I haven't had in years."

Maxwell felt his anger bubbling up again, but what was tamping it down this time was an overwhelming sense of sadness. "You slept with Marty because I told you I wanted to run for mayor?"

Annie looked past him. "Believe that if it makes this easier for you, Maxwell."

Maxwell took several seconds before speaking again, unsure how his voice was going to come out. "Why are you telling me this now?"

Annie's tone was as cold as he'd ever heard it. "For the real reason it happened. For the reason you refuse to understand."

"Then explain it to me now," he said, caught in a battle with his warring emotions.

Annie stood. "If you don't understand it now, I can't explain it to you."

She walked away then. Maxwell didn't go after her or try in any way to get more information.

Instead, he fell back into the sofa, feeling as though he'd been pushed.

~

A little before seven-thirty the next morning, Maxwell was wide awake in bed, as he had been for at least two hours. After Annie dropped the bomb on him last night, he stayed up until after midnight wondering if he was going to be able to sleep at all, if he could even get into bed next to the woman who'd pierced him so deeply. He'd considered not coming to bed last night, but there was a finality to his sleeping in the guest room that he wasn't quite ready to commit to. Eventually, he did climb in next to Annie ("next to" being a relative term). Surprisingly, he fell asleep quickly, but around five-thirty, he woke up as though he'd been jostled. He tried to will himself back to sleep — he had a monster weekend related to the campaign with several appearances scheduled — but none of his usual tricks worked. Instead, he tape-looped the conversation with Annie, specifically her revelation about her affair with Marty. Annie hadn't been specific about how long the extramarital relationship had gone on, but it hardly mattered. That his wife was capable of sleeping with another man even once signaled a level of breakdown in their marriage that Maxwell was having a tremendous amount of difficulty reconciling.

Most of the time that he lay in bed, he focused exclusively on this news. Eventually, though, he began to pull back from it. It was easy to think of the affair as the cause of all of their problems. He ultimately had to acknowledge, though, that it was a symptom. If he believed Annie that she didn't hook up with Marty until after their twentieth reunion, then the issues in their marriage had already been there. They'd been evident in Annie's complaints about feeling tethered to Joey and their home. It was clear in her reaction to his pondering a run for mayor and even more evident in her reaction to his decision to do so. That brought him back to the place he was before he learned about Annie and Marty, to that place where he wondered if it were possible to merge his desires for his life with Annie's desires for a life other than the one she was currently living. There was new information now, though. Did it change everything? Maxwell wasn't sure, but right now it felt as though it might.

As he lay there, he felt Annie stir on the other side of the bed. They were on decidedly opposite sides of the bed, so much so that Maxwell could barely feel her getting up, even though he was completely awake.

When he heard drawers opening and Annie stepping into her closet, he turned and sat up. She was fully dressed when she came out of the closet, and she startled slightly to see him looking in her direction.

"Are you going out?" Maxwell said.

Annie looked away. "It's your morning with Joey."

"I know that. You do remember that I have that store-opening thing at two, right?"

Annie's brow furrowed. "You never told me about that."

"Of course I told you about it. I put it on our joint calendar as soon as it came up."

Annie squinted at him as though she'd never heard of their joint calendar. Other than that, she didn't react.

"Are you going to be back by the early afternoon?"

Annie's expression was blank. "I seriously doubt it."

Maxwell felt his blood pressure rising. "I can't take Joey with me to this thing."

"Call one of your sisters. They're always there for you and they actually think your being mayor is a good idea."

It amazed Maxwell that there was no sense of contrition coming from Annie. How do you tell someone what she told him last night and not feel the tiniest bit apologetic or at least sheepish?

Annie turned to go into the bathroom and Maxwell sat back against his pillow. It was then that he noticed Joey standing in the doorway. How long had he been standing there? Had he witnessed the tense exchange between Maxwell and Annie? Maxwell reached an arm toward him and the boy bounced up on the bed. He bounced twice on the mattress and then did a seat drop onto Maxwell's legs, laughing as he did so. He got up and started bouncing again, this time dropping perilously close to Maxwell's groin. Joey seemed to be enjoying himself, so Maxwell tried not to inhibit him, but he did move his left hand to serve a more protective role there. Joey started bouncing again, and this time landed squarely on Maxwell's stomach. A year and a half ago, this might not have felt like much, but the kid weighed thirty-five pounds now, and thirty-five pounds with velocity felt an awful lot like a punch to the gut. An actual one, as opposed to the metaphorical one he'd received last night.

Maxwell pulled Joey into a bear hug before the boy could jump up again.

"You're gonna break dad if you keep jumping like that, Pinball," Maxwell said, laughing.

Joey wriggled out of his grip and sat on his legs frowning.

"I'm not yelling at you; I just wanted you to know that it hurts when you jump on someone's stomach."

159

Joey started wailing. Just like that. From bouncing and giggling to screaming as though he'd slammed his head on Maxwell's nightstand. By this point, Maxwell shouldn't have been surprised by this, but it still caught him completely off guard. He reached for his son and Joey, still screaming, jumped off the bed and ran down the hall. Maxwell followed Joey into his bedroom, where he found the boy in the corner of his room next to the giant Elmo, screeching, the pitch growing increasingly higher as Maxwell approached.

Maxwell sat on the floor maybe five feet from his son. "Everything's okay, Joe. I'm not hurt. There's nothing wrong."

Joey's screaming increased in volume again.

"What's going on in here?"

Maxwell turned to see Annie, fully dressed and fully made up, standing in the doorway.

"It's this thing again. He just lost it. What do you do when this happens?"

Annie looked at him as though he was an underachieving assistant. "It never happens with me. This only happens when you're around."

Maxwell was still facing Annie, but he could hear that Joey had stopped screaming. Joey *did* calm down as soon as Annie was standing in the doorway. She was clearly a calming influence on him. Maxwell might be having trouble respecting anything else about her at this point, but he had to respect that.

But was Maxwell himself an agitator? Was he responsible in some way for his child's discomfort? Knowing how he felt about the kid, Maxwell had never given this even a second's thought.

He turned to Joey now. The boy was heaving, but he seemed to be regaining his equilibrium.

"I'm going," Annie said.

Maxwell knew it wasn't worth taking this conversation further.

"Fine," was all he said.

Chapter 10

There was exactly one week left before the election, and there was one more debate on the docket. Maxwell realized that by this time next Tuesday, there was a very good chance he would know if he was going to be Oldham's next mayor. The outcome of the campaign was one of several unknowns in his life at this point, but unlike some of the others, there was a realistic schedule for a resolution. His life as a politician would begin in earnest or end completely seven days from now.

Once again, Sean Hopper was moderating. Mayor Bruce's camp had argued for Tim Commerford to handle the duties this time, but Mike pushed back and Bruce eventually relented. Maxwell was a little surprised that Bruce had given in, especially since Maxwell needed the debate much more than Bruce did. This might have been a concession to fairness, but might also have been an indication that Bruce was convinced he'd already won.

If Bruce was thinking that way, there was little in the early portion of the debate to suggest otherwise. Maxwell fumbled a relatively easy question about school lunches and then inexplicably offered the mayor an opportunity to extol his efforts to dramatically improve conditions at a failing senior center. Maxwell's positions on education and elder care were two areas where he'd scored well in the polls, so ceding this turf to the incumbent was ominous.

With his next question, Hopper moved on to the future of Oldham's economy.

"Mr. Mayor, Oldham has thrived for decades on its ability to draw visitors to its New England charm. One might even say that quaintness is our chief selling point. However, as the world changes around us, there are indications that quaintness won't be enough to keep Oldham strong. What would you do to address this if you're elected to another term?"

Though Bruce would get the opportunity to answer the question first, Maxwell knew this was a key opportunity for him. Polls had indicated that voters believed he was more on top of the future than the incumbent, and Maxwell knew that even some people in Bruce's camp were concerned that the mayor was becoming increasingly out of touch.

The mayor took a moment to begin his answer. "Well, Sean, that is an excellent question, maybe *the* question of the second half of this decade for our town. And I can assure the people of Oldham that my team has been considering this very thing for quite some time and we have begun to act on it. It's all about expanding our business base. It's about looking forward four years, eight years, twenty years and determining what Oldham can offer and what our residents and our visitors will expect from us in that future."

It was a completely vacuous answer — a politician's answer. It was the kind of thing that Maxwell would have expected from Bruce, who probably hadn't discussed anything with his staff for the last year other than the easiest path to securing another term.

Sean offered Maxwell the opportunity for a rebuttal. Seeing the chance to rally from his early flubs, Maxwell stood tall up to the mic.

"Sean, I think the people of Oldham deserve a few more specifics on a subject as important as this one. To me, the way Oldham adjusts to the needs of our times is by recruiting businesses that offer Oldham a contemporary enhancement while also underscoring the commitment to innovation and artisanship for which our town is already known. This is why I've been working to bring visionary tech companies to our office buildings and renowned restaurateurs to our commercial districts."

"I'm sure my opponent has our community's best interests in mind," Bruce said, cutting into Maxwell's allotted time. "However, no expansion of Oldham's base can come at the price of our integrity. As some of you might know, my office is currently looking into the legitimacy of one of the deals Mr. Gold agreed to."

Maxwell could barely believe that Bruce was playing this card again. Did the incumbent really think that Maxwell was so weak that he wouldn't have learned from his earlier humiliation?

"Sean, I believe I'm still on the clock," Maxwell said.

Hopper seemed a little flustered over being called on his inability to "moderate." "Yes, that is correct."

"Thanks. I'm fine, though, with sharing the rest of my time with the mayor, because I have a question for him."

Maxwell turned toward Bruce. "Mr. Mayor, I just want to make sure that everyone watching this understands exactly what you're saying when you talk about what your office is 'looking into.' Your review is not based on any evidence whatsoever that I did anything illegal in the recruitment of Sabores, correct?"

If the mayor felt challenged, his expression didn't betray it. "Mr. Gold, we've had this conversation before. You know that I can't comment on an ongoing investigation."

"But you can answer this question for the people of Oldham: isn't it true that every deal of this sort undergoes a review by your legal department?"

Bruce hesitated an instant before answering, and Maxwell could practically see the man calculating how much spin to put on his response. "Yes, every deal does undergo a review by my legal department. Needless to say, some deals require more extensive review than others."

"But not this deal."

Bruce first turned toward the audience, then toward Sean Hopper, and finally toward Maxwell. In each case, he expressed impatience. "As I've said more times than I possibly should need to, Mr. Gold, I can't comment on an ongoing investigation."

Maxwell moved closer to the mic. "And if this were in fact an ongoing investigation, I would understand. However, this one is not ongoing. My office received notification on Friday from your legal department that the Sabores deal had cleared the review process. You are aware, I assume, that the Chamber of Commerce is notified whenever a new business is given clearance."

"Yes, of course, I'm aware of that."

"So then there's no ongoing investigation into the recruitment of Sabores."

Bruce seemed to be attempting to glower without coming off as angry to the cameras. "If the legal department sent out the notice on Friday, then there is no ongoing investigation about which I am aware. I'm sure you can understand, Mr. Gold, that an awful lot of paperwork goes past my desk." He chuckled thinly. "If you want to be mayor, I certainly hope you've checked into how much work is involved."

"I'm ready for the work, Mr. Mayor. And I appreciate your clarifying that the work I did in recruiting a nationally acclaimed restaurateur to Oldham was done completely above board." Maxwell turned to the moderator. "Sean, I assume I can have the rest of my time to complete my response to the mayor's original statement?"

Sean gathered himself. "Technically, you used that time to engage Mayor Bruce in this exchange. However, my next question for you was to ask how you would deal with the same issue of Oldham's future, so feel free to answer that question now."

Maxwell hadn't felt this "in the pocket" since the campaign began. He knew he'd stung Bruce — and he'd done so without resorting to innuendo or negativity — and he had the opportunity right now to follow up on that by delivering a message that he believed in very strongly.

"Thank you, Sean. As you know, I've lived in Oldham most of my life. I understand the fabric of this community, and I understand what makes our town exceptional. People talk about how our location on the Connecticut River Valley makes us the ideal location for leaf-peeping in the fall, and I know I'm not in the minority of people around here who consider October to be their favorite month of the year. But what people talk about less is the effect our location has on our culture. We are close enough to New York and Boston — two of the most progressive and sophisticated cities in the world — to benefit from their influence. And we are also deep enough into the open spaces of eastern Connecticut that we have the charm and personal scale of a great New England village. This combination makes Oldham the place we are proud to call home. And as we evolve into the future, we need to maintain that combination, not by holding fast to what we already are, but by following the natural progression of what we are to be."

Maxwell hadn't planned on turning this into a speech, but the words were falling from his lips as easily as if he'd practiced this in front of a mirror for days. He allowed himself a quick glance at the audience and got the sense that people were paying attention. Even Sean seemed locked into what he was saying.

"For this reason, we want to recruit businesses to Oldham that embrace our signature qualities of sophistication and human scale. This is why I've already been working aggressively to bring creative shops to the tech plaza. This is why I've been seeking to fill our emerging Restaurant Row with first-class chefs. It is why I have a plan to incentivize our local artisans to extend their footprint globally through the Internet, and why I have another plan in place to offer next-generation marketing and merchandising support to our current merchants.

"Oldham has never seen a commercial initiative on this scale, and I am convinced that it will allow us to evolve exactly the way we need to evolve while allowing us to maintain the identity we already love."

Maxwell stepped back from the mic, feeling very satisfied with his ability to get his message across. He felt even more satisfied when Sean asked Bruce for a rebuttal and the mayor responded, "It seems to me we've already spent enough time on this topic. Let's move on."

They did move on, but it hardly mattered to Maxwell. As the debate continued, he felt that he scored points even in areas where Bruce had clear strengths, like traffic, security, and the budget. When the debate ended, the mayor's eyes narrowed as he shook Maxwell's hand. Maxwell read that as the incumbent's way of saying "nice job."

The mayor went off to hug his wife. Maxwell's wife was of course too far away to hug, in more ways than one. He had to satisfy himself with handshakes from Mike and Alecia.

"You know, the resemblance is uncanny," Mike said to Alecia.

Maxwell had no idea what Mike was talking about. "Resemblance?"

"To Maxwell Gold. You really do look *just like him*."

"I'm not sure if I should feel complimented or insulted by that comment, Mike."

"I absolutely meant it as a compliment. Nice job of showing up tonight."

Maxwell laughed. "Do you think it'll make any difference?"

"I guess we'll find out in a week."

∽

Maxwell had heard that, by the time your kid reached the age of three, you could relax, at least a little bit. The endless vigilance required of minding a toddler lessened as the

171

child proved less likely to stick a fork in an electrical outlet or use a pair of scissors as an action figure. Maybe Joey was perhaps a little behind on the developmental curve in this regard, because Maxwell still didn't feel he could take his eye from him for very long. His "Pinball" nickname was still valid, and that required extra attention.

Still, Maxwell felt relatively sanguine about going into the kitchen for another cup of coffee while Joey was playing with a truck on the floor of the den. Yes, he could probably run over his hand with the truck, and that might hurt a bit, but there were no choking hazards on the truck and Joey was — mostly — unlikely to get a concussion from banging himself in the head with the vehicle.

Maxwell was in the kitchen maybe forty-five seconds. He poured coffee into his mug from the carafe and went to the refrigerator to add a splash of half-and-half. He'd kept his ears tuned to the den the entire time. As he began to walk back into that room, though, he heard a sound he wasn't expecting to hear. It sounded like creaking.

He quickened his pace and found the truck where it had been when he left. Joey, however, was not there. He heard the creaking again and turned toward a bookshelf in the corner of the room — to see that his son had climbed nearly to the top. There were two problems with this. One was that Joey could fall and hurt himself very badly. The other was that the bookshelf was not bolted to the wall. It was heavily weighted with books and unlikely to come down, but with a three-year-old perched precariously on it, who knew what might happen? And if the bookshelf tumbled, it would crush Joey.

Maxwell had the presence of mind not to yell to his son, since doing so might have caused the boy to startle and tumble to the floor. Instead, he moved quickly to the bookshelf, figuring he could catch Joey or keep the shelf up against the wall. From this spot, he was able to reach Joey, and he grabbed the boy around the waist and pulled him to his chest.

Joey was laughing when Maxwell pulled him down, but then he looked at his father's face and started crying — the fire alarm cry that had become an all-too-common sound in this house. Maxwell brought him over to the couch and sat the boy on his lap.

"Joey, what were you thinking?" Maxwell said as his butt hit the seat.

Joey just cried harder.

"We've talked about the bookshelves. You know that climbing up on them can be very, very dangerous."

Joey's sobbing lessened enough for him to bawl out, "So?"

"So? So you could get really hurt. You know that's what dangerous means."

"I wanna get hurt." Joey wailed this, as though he were revealing his darkest secret.

"What? Joey, what are you talking about?"

Joey had certainly shown an inclination toward destructiveness in his young life, but Maxwell had never interpreted this as *self*-destructiveness. Was this another one of the demons that had been haunting his son in the past year? Did the problems they'd been facing go beyond behavioral issues and into truly dangerous ones?

It was going to take a while to find out, because Joey ratcheted up his wailing. It was so loud, Maxwell was sure it was audible down the block. Maxwell pulled the boy closer to him and let him cry it out.

Joey was still sitting in Maxwell's lap a couple of minutes later when he calmed down.

"Joe, why were you saying that you wanted to get hurt?"

He pointed to the television. "Tommy get hurt."

Maxwell assumed that Tommy was a character on one of the shows Joey watched, though he couldn't think of a Tommy right now.

"You wanted to get hurt because Tommy got hurt?"

Joey nodded.

"Joe, you know that TV things and real-life things are different, right?"

Joey nodded again. "Tommy mommy and daddy fight."

Maxwell drew his son closer. "What?"

"Tommy mommy and daddy fight. Tommy get hurt and they don't fight no more."

Maxwell actually felt a chill run down his back. "You're saying that you wanted to get hurt because Mommy and Daddy have been fighting?"

"Mommy and Daddy fight *a lot*."

Maxwell had no idea that Joey had noticed how tense things had gotten between himself and Annie. This was foolish of him, of course. Kids notice everything and things had been *very* tense. But by putting this in context, some of the key mysteries surrounding Joey's behavior began to reveal themselves. Joey's hair-trigger tantrums, his sudden tendency toward destructiveness, his long bouts of inconsolable crying — these had all begun to happen in the last year when things started to get bad enough in Maxwell and Annie's marriage that they had started to bleed through into their everyday lives.

Maxwell had been concerned that something might be wrong with his son. Instead, he should have been concerned about how something that was wrong with himself was affecting his son.

He kissed Joey on the head. "Mommy and Daddy don't want you to get hurt for us, Joey. Please don't do anything that dangerous again. We'll stop fighting; I promise."

Maxwell wasn't sure how he was going to make good on that promise, but he knew it was absolutely essential that he do so.

Chapter 11

It dawned on Maxwell that no one had prepped him on what to do on the day of an election. Of course, he got to the polls when they opened so the media could take shots of him casting his ballot. Annie even surprised him by coming along with Joey. She didn't reveal who she voted for and Maxwell decided not to ask. There hadn't been much conversation between them since Annie revealed her affair with Marty. This wasn't simply a case of Maxwell allowing negative emotions to fester; he literally had no idea how to talk to his wife now.

After voting, there wasn't much Maxwell could do. Mike had told him that he was allowed to stand outside of polling places — as long as he maintained a certain distance from the polls themselves — to greet voters, but that seemed pathetic to him. Annie had gone off to a "mommy and me" gymnastics session with Joey, not that spending the day with her was a realistic option. Maxwell had cleared his calendar, since he didn't think he'd be very effective in meetings today, but he went to the office anyway. It was some-place to be, and if nothing else, he could busy himself with paperwork until 3:00 when it was time for him to head down to campaign headquarters.

The results of the final opinion poll prior to the election were inconclusive. It was clear that Maxwell had won the last debate; most of those asked said he'd done so decisively. What was far less clear was whether he'd swayed enough voters. According to the poll, he was still trailing, but the deficit was with-in the margin of error. Maybe he *should* be out there shaking hands. If he didn't and he lost by eighteen votes, he would berate him-self for failing to give the campaign every-thing he had in the end. However, if he did and he still lost by a slim margin, he would berate himself for resorting to such obvious pandering on the final day. In the end, he de-cided that it was probably more appropriate for him to stay in his office signing expense account forms. It was extremely unlikely that the race was going to come down to eighteen votes.

A little before noon, Maria came by and suggested they go out for lunch. Maxwell found that he was reluctant to go out to a restaurant, knowing that he'd encounter any number of people who'd want him to predict the outcome of the election. Instead, they called in for sandwiches to eat at the table in his office.

"You know, this is a nice office," Maria said as she pulled the food from the bag. "I don't know that I ever paid attention to how nice this place is. Is the mayor's office this nice?"

Maxwell pulled a couple of bottles of sparkling water from his refrigerator and brought them to the table. "It's gorgeous. Detailed molding, huge, antique desk, built-in bookshelves. It looks like the kind of place the chairman of a university history department would have."

"Sounds way too sophisticated for Jack Bruce."

Maxwell chuckled. "Yeah, I should have run on the I-fit-the-office-better platform. Where were you when I needed you?"

They sat down to eat, clinking bottles in a silent toast before taking their first bites.

"Are you ready for this?" Maria said.

"Which part?"

"Pick one. The waiting for the results part. The becoming mayor part. The *not* becoming mayor part."

Maxwell shrugged. "As ready as I can be. I'm finding this bit of it a little unnerving, to tell you the truth. I feel like I'm standing on stage and I don't know what to do with my hands. And I think I'll be okay if I don't win.

There was always a very real chance of that, right? Winning would definitely be better, though."

"You mean you weren't just campaigning for the last year for the fun of it?"

This got a laugh out of him. "Yeah, it was either this or taking up golf." He took a sip of his drink and then continued. "No, you know, I really do want this. I think it crystallized for me over the course of the campaign. At first, it just seemed like a smart career move. I mean, how long can you be president of the Chamber of Commerce, right? But then as we started developing the platform, I realized that this was about playing a part in the future. I don't think I fully understood how much that mattered to me until now."

Maria unwrapped her sandwich. "Yeah, I get that."

"That and, if I can get Bruce to show me some of his tricks, we can get a bunch of renovations on the house for a huge discount."

Maria laughed surprisingly loudly, which caused Maxwell to laugh as well.

She took a drink from her bottle. "And Annie's made peace with your shaping the future?"

Maxwell studied his lunch. "I think the words 'Annie' and 'peace' are a bit of a contradiction right now."

Maria cringed. "Does that mean she's making calls at Bruce headquarters right now?"

"Nah, Annie hates politics."

"How much strain is your becoming mayor going to put on your marriage?"

Maxwell scoffed. "Going to? Probably not a whole lot more than it already has."

Maria poked at her cole slaw. It seemed that neither of them were terribly interested in making eye contact at this point. If Maxwell were going to tell anyone about Annie's infidelity, it would be Maria, but he was still staying loyal to that notion that you didn't share the ugly parts of your marriage with your family.

"Have you thought this all the way through?" she said.

Maxwell waited a few seconds before responding. "There were some variables I might not have factored into the equation."

"How are you going to deal with that?"

He picked up a half of his sandwich. "I guess we'll all find out soon, huh?"

Maxwell offered his sister a complicated smile and she returned it with one that wasn't complicated at all. They finished their lunch a few minutes later, and Maxwell rose to clean things up. As he did, Maria got up with him.

"I'm gonna get going. Unless you need me to prevent you from driving your staff crazy."

"That's okay; my staff is already crazy."

"I'll come by the campaign headquarters about six. Let me know if you hear anything before then."

She kissed him on the cheek and gave him a longer hug than she usually offered while she was saying goodbye. Maxwell almost asked her to stay, suggesting coffee or a card game — anything to make the next few hours speed by. Instead, he went back to his desk.

∽

At 2:30, having tinkered around his office as long as he could, Maxwell left for the campaign headquarters. He'd left the office in the middle of the day several times over the course of the campaign, but saying goodnight to his staff this time felt different. In many ways, it felt like saying goodbye. Maybe, in fact, he was doing exactly that. Certainly, if he won the election today, he would be leaving the Chamber, and one of the conditions under which the Chamber allowed him to run while still holding his position was that he wouldn't take any staff with him for at least a year. What had begun creeping into his mind over the past few days, though, was that it might be time to leave even if he lost. Maxwell liked this work and he was proud of what he'd been able to accomplish here, but there was only so much he could accomplish from this position. Hartford was within commuting distance. Providence was only a little farther away. Maybe it was time to find out if there was something available for him at one of these state capitals. Affecting policy had gotten into his blood; if he couldn't have a bigger job in a smaller venue like Oldham, maybe it was time to consider a smaller (or at least equivalent) spot in a bigger one.

Maxwell hadn't really considered this in this way until now, but he'd just become conscious of the fact that his mind had been working on it in the background. Maybe that's why leaving his office today felt so different. He was coming to the end of an important and cherished juncture in his life.

His campaign team applauded when he walked into the headquarters, which startled him a bit. They'd certainly never done that before. Had they received some good news that Mike was anxious to share? That turned out not to be the case.

"The exit polling is completely inconclusive," his campaign manager said as the two walked to Mike's office.

"I guess it was a little too much to hope that all of our other polls had been wrong and that we actually had a commanding lead, huh?"

Steve had been trailing behind them. "We're right within the margin of error, which means this is likely to stay close all night. In fact, I think it's likely that you'll do better with later voters than you have with early ones. Bruce probably has a considerable advantage over you with commuters."

Maxwell thought that Steve might have been spending far too much time with his numbers. He understood the theory — that he was the champion of the local merchant and that they voted at the end of the business day rather than the beginning — but it was nothing more than a supposition.

Mike and Maxwell sat at opposite ends of Mike's couch, while Steve pulled up a chair from Mike's desk.

"What are we supposed to do between now and when the polls close?" Maxwell said.

Mike pointed toward the desks outside his office. "Well, they're still working the phones pretty hard. The job at this point is to guilt people who are likely to vote for you into getting into their cars and driving to their polling places. We don't want to lose this thing because people who would have voted for you couldn't bother to pull the lever.

Meanwhile, are you sure you don't want to go shake a few hands outside of a couple of venues?"

Maxwell shook his head. "I get the phone calls. But what's the point of my going out into town to beg for votes on Election Day? Does anybody actually go to vote without knowing who they're going to be voting for?"

"No, not many."

"So then back to the original question: what are *we* supposed to do today."

They both looked at Steve, who was reading a report on his iPad. There was little question that Steve would find a way to keep himself busy until the polls closed.

"Sit on our hands," Mike said. "Try not to let the uncertainty freak us out."

"In other words do what I've been doing since I got up this morning. At least I've been doing the right thing."

Mike chuckled and the three of them sat quietly for a few minutes, Steve continuing to read his reports and Maxwell studying the carpet.

"I saw that Annie came out to vote with you this morning," Mike said. "That was good. Is she going to be coming by later?"

Maxwell shrugged. "Have you ever seen her here?"

"We haven't had Election Day before."

Maxwell arched an eyebrow. "I think it would be one of the bigger surprises of my life if she did."

Mike nodded slowly, as though he was processing Maxwell's subtext. "She's coming to the Sugar Maple later, though, right?"

The inn, which the Gold family had owned until last year, had agreed to host the campaign's election night festivities.

"It's within the margin of error," Maxwell said.

A little after four, Alecia joined them. "Anything on the exit polls?" she said.

Mike gave her the same information he'd already given Maxwell.

Alecia absorbed this while she settled into the chair Steve had occupied. Maxwell hadn't noticed until now that Alecia and Steve rarely stayed in the same space for long. He wondered if it would have been important to see that earlier. "I've been tapping into my network all day, getting people from outside of Oldham to communicate with people who live in Oldham asking about the election."

Maxwell was fascinated with how Alecia's mind worked. He would definitely need to stay in touch with her after the election. There was much he could learn from her.

"Interesting," Mike said. "Someone calls you or messages you and says, 'What's happening in your mayoral race?' and it gives the impression that the race is a much bigger deal than you might have thought it was."

Alecia smiled at Mike. "That's the theory, anyway. We're getting a lot of pings on it. Every little thing can make a difference in a race this tight." She turned to Maxwell. "How are you holding up?"

"I'm a little restless. A lot restless, really. Other than that, I'm surprisingly fine. I'm just ready to find out how this is going to work out."

"What's your gut telling you?"

Maxwell allowed himself a few seconds to address that question honestly. "I think it's going to work out okay."

Alecia reached out and patted him on the knee. "Me too. I definitely think it's going to work out okay."

She startled as though someone had just stuck her in the back with a pin. "I just had another idea. Gotta get to my laptop."

With that, she was out of Mike's office, Maxwell admiringly watching her retreat.

He looked back at Mike. "Do you feel a little guilty that other people are working while we're just sitting on our hands?"

"Not in the least. You?"

"No, not really."

~⌣

Maxwell had not been inside the Sugar Maple Inn for more than a year. The inn had changed ownership the day after the last of their family's annual Halloween parties, and while his curiosity spiked every time he drove by the place, he hadn't chosen to visit. There had been some talk about the new owners maintaining the Halloween party tradition, but it hadn't come to pass. Halloween — a signal event in the Gold household for nearly Maxwell's entire life — had been a blur for him this year, between the election, the situation with Annie, and Maxwell's growing concern that their toxicity was poisoning their son. Annie had taken Joey trick-or-treating in the neighborhood before he got home from work, and beyond Joey's having three peanut butter cups for dinner and the sleeping in his Scooby-Doo costume, October 31 was a non-event for Maxwell this time.

He'd been a bit surprised when the Sugar Maple reached out to offer to host Maxwell's election night event, because the owners had no actual ties to Oldham. They operated a national network of bed and breakfasts, and the managers of the Sugar Maple had been brought in from another of the consortium's locations in Maine. Of course, it was a great payday for them and very good publicity as well, so maybe this was just a function of some marketing person in the corporate office doing his homework.

Maxwell noticed that they'd done very little to change the place. Some of the walls seemed freshly painted and there was a much more prominent rack of literature for nearby attractions in the lobby, but otherwise the Sugar Maple seemed just as the Golds had left it. Realizing this led to an ambush of melancholy that Maxwell immediately sought to tamp down. His emotions were already surging; if he got overly sentimental right now, it might truly paralyze him.

When he got there a little before seven, he walked directly into the dining room where others had already gathered. For the second time that day, he entered a room to applause. He could get used to something like that. At least he thought he could. He waved to everyone and thanked them for coming.

His eyes landed on his sister Deborah, who'd been a fixture in this room for more than a decade. It seemed so natural to see her here, even though she wasn't wearing her chef's whites.

"How many times have you started walking into the kitchen?" he said as he walked over to her.

Deborah laughed at the question. "I'm perfectly capable of distinguishing between the present and the past, thank you." She paused for a beat and then added, "I've only done it four or five times."

Appetizers were being passed and someone handed him a glass of Champagne, which seemed terribly premature. Thinking that he'd rather not be drinking at all right now, he exchanged it for a glass of sparkling water.

There were television monitors in every corner of the room, and a stage had been set up and dressed with a large "Gold for Mayor" banner. Election coverage was going strong on the monitors, two of which were tuned to the local cable news station, one of which carried a station out of Hartford, and a fourth of which was broadcasting national election details. Maxwell paid the monitors little mind, even though he'd been following a couple of gubernatorial battles in the national news. As far as his race was concerned, he had better information than any of the broadcasters, and he knew that exit polling had continued to be inconclusive throughout the day. He continued to be slightly behind the incumbent, but well within the margin of error.

Surprising him for the second time that day, Annie showed up a few minutes later with Joey in her arms. The kid received a bigger round of applause than Maxwell had, which caused Joey to hide his face in his mother's shoulder. Annie looked gorgeous in a cobalt cocktail dress, and it once again registered on Maxwell that his wife always looked beautiful to him, regardless of the circumstances. He wondered if that would always be the case, though if he could admire the way she looked now, maybe he always would.

Annie surprised him further by locking eyes with him and moving in his direction. Joey reached out for him as they got closer, and Maxwell took him in his arms and twirled him, eliciting a high-pitched giggle from the boy.

"Any news yet?" Annie said.

"Nothing meaningful. Way too close to call."

"Well, you knew you weren't going to run away with it."

"That I definitely knew. What I wasn't sure about was whether Bruce would just wipe the floor with me."

"That was never going to happen," Annie said expressing more confidence in him than he'd come to expect.

That was easily the longest exchange between them since Annie had dropped the bomb on him. There was something very natural in Annie's tone, as though it was entirely normal for them to be chatting this way.

Maxwell couldn't process this right now, but he would file it away for later.

For the next several minutes, various photographers took shots of Maxwell, Annie, and Joey. Maxwell kept waiting for the point when Annie would start complaining, but she just kept smiling and offering support for him, saying the kinds of things it would have been great for her to say at the last fundraiser. *This is what it could have been like the entire campaign,* Maxwell thought. Annie actually seemed to be enjoying herself. Why had she been so unwilling to give this a chance earlier? Why was she doing it now? Ever since Annie had revealed her infidelity and even more since Joey revealed his "solution" to their tensions, Maxwell had been thinking about where things went from here. That wasn't something he could think about now, though. There were too many hands to shake, too many people to thank. And then, of course, there was the evening's biggest unknown — the election results.

The polls closed at 9:00, and the official numbers started to trickle in. As expected, there was nothing definitive in the early numbers. Fifteen minutes later, Annie told him that she was going home, saying that she needed to get Joey to bed. Joey seemed to be holding up very well, especially since he was getting so much attention from aunts, uncles, and friends of the family, and Maxwell mentioned this to his wife. She wasn't swayed.

"I'm pretty used up for the night," Annie said, and Maxwell interpreted this to mean that these past two hours had been all she had been willing to offer. Annie had actually surprised him enough by coming that he felt a twinge of disappointment before going to kiss his son goodnight. By the time Annie left the dining room, the disappointment had faded completely.

That left the waiting. Oldham had a half-dozen voting precincts, and they were of varying levels of efficiency in terms of delivering results. The first two that reported had Bruce ahead by four points. The third, the precinct that included the Hickory commercial district, the town's biggest, delivered numbers strong enough to put Maxwell in the lead by a little more than a point.

"This could happen," Mike said when he delivered this information.

Maxwell tried not to let the excitement overwhelm him. "You mean I might actually have to be mayor? I thought we were just goofing around. I have absolutely no plan for tomorrow."

Steve had been trailing behind Mike, iPad in hand. "The three precincts that haven't reported yet are in southeast Oldham, the commercial/residential area out by Birch, and the waterfront. Southeast is going to wipe out all of this lead, but if you don't get hit too hard there, the other two districts should look pretty good for you."

Maxwell laughed inwardly at the tactlessness of Steve's analysis, even as he agreed with most of it. He was least certain about what would happen in the waterfront district, Oldham's wealthiest. Lots of Bruce cronies lived there.

By eleven, the southeast had reported, and Maxwell was down again by two points. Bruce's people started calling for a concession at that stage, claiming their exit polling had the mayor winning the other two precincts handily, but the polling numbers from Maxwell's camp didn't tell the same story, so Maxwell refused.

Birch came in about a half-hour later, and it hadn't delivered as heavily for Maxwell as he had hoped. He was still trailing by nearly a point. With one precinct remaining, he needed to pick up about four hundred and fifty votes. The math didn't seem good to him, but he called Mike, Steve, and Alecia together.

"Is there any chance we could make up that margin?" he said.

Steve flipped through a handful of different scenarios on his iPad. "I don't see how."

Maxwell had been assuming as much. He looked first to Alecia and then Mike for confirmation. Both said they agreed with Steve.

Maxwell nodded slowly. "Hey, we kept Bruce sweating for a long time. That's never happened in any of his other campaigns."

Mike clapped him on the shoulder and then, catching Maxwell off guard, pulled him close for a hug. "I'm proud of you. You ran like a winner."

The sentiment warmed Maxwell. He held the hug a moment longer and then said, "I guess I'd better go call the mayor."

He pulled out his phone and walked into the hallway outside of the kitchen, away from the crowd. Though a number of people had left the Sugar Maple, there was still a considerable crowd there, and it was much too noisy for a phone call.

He was connected with Bruce immediately.

"Congratulations, Mr. Mayor. It looks like you've won yourself another term."

"I always assumed I'd win, Gold."

Maxwell closed his eyes and tried not to react to Bruce's smugness. "Well, you did, Mr. Mayor, so again, congratulations."

"Appreciated, Gold. Anything else?"

"No, I'm sure you have a speech to deliver. As do I."

Maxwell hung up. He'd actually imagined this moment, but it had always seemed less empty than what he got in reality. He took a deep breath before turning to head back into the dining room. When he did, he saw Alecia standing by the door.

"Let me guess: Bruce stayed classy, right?" she said.

Maxwell laughed thinly. "As classy as ever."

"You can't believe you lost to this guy, can you?"

"Yeah, I guess. I just don't understand why this town — a town filled with smart, open-minded people — keep voting for a boor like Bruce. I don't know; maybe it's because in a lot of ways it really doesn't matter. The people here are so capable and resourceful that maybe it doesn't matter who's mayor."

Alecia took a step closer. "That's exactly what I want to talk to you about."

"About how I shouldn't have been trying to be mayor in the first place?"

She smiled at him softly. "Not that exactly. I just think that you actually want to accomplish something, Maxwell. If you'd been elected, you would almost certainly have kept Oldham moving forward. You might have even turned it into a model community of its size. But there's a very real chance that Oldham will accomplish that on its own — and more to the point, it's likely to thrive even with a boor like Bruce at the helm. I don't think Oldham is your platform."

Maxwell had been considering the same thing earlier, but he didn't think it was appropriate to share this with Alecia right now. "It's not?"

"It's not. Your platform is Thrive America."

Maxwell had heard the name before, but it took him several seconds to register where. "Those guys who came to the Chamber offices to talk about the possibility of space in the tech center?"

"We're signing a lease next week."

Maxwell arched an eyebrow. "We?"

Alecia smiled again. She seemed more relaxed than Maxwell had ever seen her, and he'd seen her often over the past few months. "Thrive America is my baby. The people you met with are my CIO and CTO."

This information was not easy to process given that Maxwell was still trying to process his loss. "You run a party-planning business *and* a think tank?"

"It's not as incongruous as it sounds. The methodologies and the algorithms that I've used to build the party-planning business — the same ones I used to help you with your campaign — align surprisingly well with what we want to accomplish with Thrive America."

"Which is?"

"We want to offer entrepreneurs and organizations the best possible set of tools for success by giving them the advantage of our technology and our scale."

Surprisingly, Maxwell found himself back in business mode. "That's got to be a huge undertaking. Who's backing you?"

"We don't need backing." Alecia offered a coy expression. "I'm funding this myself."

Maxwell's eyes widened. "You just happen to have a couple of dozen million lying around?"

Alecia shrugged. "I do, actually. My late husband and I did okay for ourselves in the tech boom in the mid-aughts."

Maxwell started scanning his mind again. When he landed on a reference, his surprise increased. "Your late husband was *Scott Moore*?"

Alecia gave him the slightest nod. "He was the company spokesperson. I've never been a big fan of the limelight."

Every now and then people transformed in front of Maxwell's eyes. That was happening right here with Alecia. Scott Moore and his team — led, Maxwell was guessing, by Alecia — had redefined the processing of Big Data in the first half of the last decade. They ultimately sold their technology to a huge Internet retailer for ten figures. Less than a year later, Scott Moore died in a mountain climbing accident.

"Anyway," Alecia said while Maxwell was still wrapping his mind around this, "I spent more than five years working on a new algorithm. The party-planning business was a test. I did it first in Boston and then here because I wanted to see if it would be applicable in different municipalities. Your campaign was a test, too."

Maxwell grimaced. "I hope that your party-planning business is doing better than my campaign did."

Alecia laughed. "Your campaign did great. The odds were overwhelmingly against you, though I have a feeling no one ever explained that to you. In spite of his scandals, Bruce is entrenched. And you still came within a few hundred votes of unseating him."

The idea of being that close and losing stung every time Maxwell considered it. Where could he have picked up those votes? Had his public flubs generated the losing margin? Alecia seemed to be saying that in the aggregate he'd outperformed expectations, but if he'd outperformed expectations just a little more, he could have been celebrating rather than conceding now.

"Maxwell, I want you to become CEO of Thrive America."

Maxwell snapped out of his reverie. "You what?"

"You're the right guy for the job. You have vision, ambition, and empathy. You wanted to be mayor so you could have an impact on Oldham? That's great, but how about having an impact on every Oldham in the country?"

This might have been the most surreal five minutes of Maxwell's life. He'd just gone from losing something he desperately wanted to being offered something exponentially better. Today had definitely proven to be the start of a new juncture for him. Just not the new juncture he'd expected.

"I have to go deliver a concession speech," he said. "After that, do you think I could buy you a drink?"

Chapter 12

~

Maxwell wound up speaking with Alecia until after one in the morning, and by the end of the conversation, he'd accepted the position with Thrive America. What an odd turn of events. He'd been working for more than a year toward a goal he truly believed he desired. Then, within a few hours, he'd failed to achieve that goal and found the opportunity replaced by one that excited him considerably more. He assumed that Jack Bruce was celebrating his victory with his usual old-school arrogance, whiskey, and cigars, but Maxwell came away feeling like more of a winner and especially glad that he'd never pandered or resorted to negative politics over the course of the campaign. He wouldn't need to carry around the muck of that for the rest of his life. Maxwell wondered if Bruce ever felt dirty over the way he sought his victories, but he had a feeling that the mayor didn't. Different people respond to the same situation in different ways.

Annie was of course asleep when he got home. He'd called her right before his concession speech because he didn't think it was appropriate that she learn of his loss from the television. It was clear when she answered that she'd already gone to bed. She congratulated him for running a good race, and his first reaction was to think, *How would you know that I did*? Cynicism seemed to be coming to him naturally with Annie now. He'd never considered himself to be a cynical person.

Even though he'd gotten into bed only a few hours before, he was up and in the kitchen with a cup of coffee by six. He'd fallen asleep surprisingly easily, but when he awoke, his mind started racing with thoughts of what lay ahead, and he knew that trying to get back to sleep was going to be an exercise in futility. His staff knew not to expect him at his regular time this morning, but he thought he might actually show up in the office early. He needed to resign, of course, and he'd want to be as helpful in the transition as he could before moving to his new gig. Fortunately, some of that work was already in place, including discussions about possible successors, since he would have been leaving the Chamber anyway if the election had turned out differently.

He was beginning to think about getting dressed to go into the office when he heard Joey running out of his room. The kid literally hit the ground running every single day. He wasn't one of those children who tiptoed into their parents' bedrooms when they awoke. Not Joey. He thundered; he belly-flopped.

Because Joey didn't know Maxwell was in the kitchen, the boy went to wake up his mom. Maxwell thought about going to retrieve his son, maybe giving Annie the opportunity to sleep in, but he poured himself some more coffee instead. Within five minutes, the television in the den was on and Annie was coming into the kitchen.

"I thought maybe you'd gone to the office already," she said after registering mild surprise at seeing him. She went to the refrigerator for milk for her coffee.

"I've been telling myself for the past half hour that I need to get out of this chair and get to work. I guess I really should do that, huh?"

She poured coffee and then turned to him. "Yeah, you certainly don't want to get fired now."

Maxwell thought it was possible that she was saying this as a way to start a conversation about the election results, but he also thought it was likely that she was expressing real concerns about his place in the family as a breadwinner. *You can't fail at your job now, Maxwell, not after you failed trying to become mayor. It's time for you to get back to toeing the line.*

"I have a little update on that, actually."

Annie's raised eyebrows showed that he'd gained her attention.

"You know Alecia Moore?" he said.

Annie shook her head slowly. "Which one is that?"

"She was the networking guru who joined the campaign."

Annie's expression was largely blank. "Yeah, I sort of remember. What about her?"

Even though he was still having trouble engaging in a conversation of any length with his wife, he couldn't prevent his excitement about his new opportunity from creeping into his voice. "She's unimaginably wealthy, she's a visionary, and she's starting a next-generation think tank in the tech center called Thrive America."

Annie fished a bagel from a bag on the counter and put half of it in the toaster. "Sounds interesting."

Maxwell waited until Annie finished what she was doing before he spoke again. "The interesting part is what comes next. She's asked me to become CEO of this new company."

Annie leaned against the counter. "Wow. Do you think you want to take it?"

Maxwell took a sip of his coffee. Life decisions of this sort were usually the kind of thing you discussed with your spouse first. "I've already taken it."

Annie looked down at the floor for a second before looking back up at him. "How's the pay?"

"A lot better than what the Chamber pays me, and that's before you consider equity and profit sharing."

Annie made a show of checking the status of her bagel. "Are you going to be working until three in the morning every day?"

"There might be some days like that, but not most."

The bagel came out of the toaster and Annie spread some cream cheese on it without reacting. She brought her plate and coffee cup to the table where Maxwell was sitting.

"Congratulations," she said in a measured way. "This could be good for you."

Again, Maxwell felt excitement he couldn't tamp down. "I think it will be. I didn't realize how ready I was for something like this until I heard about the job."

Annie took a bite of her bagel and looked off in the middle distance. "This could be good for us, actually. Maybe this is the kind of change we need to get back on track."

It seemed odd to Maxwell that she was saying this without looking at him. She was delivering the line, almost as though she were reading it from a Teleprompter.

There was nothing premeditated about what Maxwell did next. He supposed he'd been processing this in his subconscious since he heard about Annie's infidelity, maybe even before then. Annie's mention of this being the sort of change they needed brought it to the forefront, though. With the kind of rush of clarity that Maxwell had only experienced a few times in his life, he projected their marriage forward. He tried to imagine them a couple of years from now when Joey was in school full-time and Annie was free to use her days however she desired. He tried to imagine them a few years after that when Thrive America had gained so much value that the equity position Alecia was giving him would give them more financial freedom than they'd ever anticipated. He tried to imagine them after Joey had gone off to college, with the means to do whatever they wanted and enough youth to enjoy it.

And he saw the same thing in each image: Annie disappointed. He might have been able to forgive her for cheating on him. But he was never going to be able to let go of the fact that she'd blamed him for her dissatisfaction with her life, that she seemed more content to reinforce how miserable she was with the situation she'd found herself in and her unwillingness to accept any attempt he made to try to help her out of that situation. She would blame his new work for backing her into a corner just as she'd blamed the mayoral campaign or the rigors of his job with the Chamber. She would blame Joey for being a responsibility, even as he became less of one. She would blame their marriage for turning her into something less than the ideal for herself that she'd been constantly unwilling to share with him.

Annie was still looking away from Maxwell, which allowed him to study her for a few seconds. She was so beautiful. He might even still love her, at least on some level. But she'd spent so much time over the past couple of years being unhappy and making him feel responsible for that unhappiness, that he finally realized they were never again going to be what they once were together, and that every version of what they might become together was going to be emotionally destructive for both of them.

"I don't think we should talk about getting back on track, Annie," he said, finding more strength in his voice with every word. "I think we should talk about joint custody."

Chapter 13

~

Maxwell hadn't lived downtown on Hickory since he moved out of his parents' home at the Sugar Maple Inn. Even in the quiet of the house he was renting there now, he could sense the bustle not far from his door. He'd taken the lease on this place for a year, and he wasn't sure whether he'd stay in town once the lease was up. Things would be rolling at Thrive America and it might make more sense for him to be closer to the tech center. For now, though, being in the middle of the action was the best thing for Joey and him. The park was just down the street, excellent ice cream was two blocks away, and they were less than a five-minute walk from the best sticky buns on the planet. What more could two boys need?

Annie had responded to his request for a divorce with surprise and anger. They'd stayed at the dining room table for more than two hours that day rehashing their history, especially the past few years. As he would have anticipated if he'd known he was going to do it, Maxwell heard a great deal of blaming from Annie, along with some revisionist history. Marty Balin's name didn't come up.

By the next day, though, Annie seemed as though she had begun to accept things. She talked about the need to rediscover herself and vowed not to make Joey a pawn in their separation. Maxwell guessed that he'd shocked her — this was understandable, because he'd also shocked himself — and that once Annie began to process what he'd said to her, she also began to realize that splitting was probably the best course of action.

Maxwell didn't kid himself that this was the best thing for Joey. The best thing for Joey was to grow up in a household where his parents loved and supported each other. However, Maxwell was convinced that this was the best thing for Joey under the circumstances. Maxwell knew what it was like to love Annie and to be loved by her, and what they'd been living with the past couple of years felt like a pale imitation. What was even more obvious was that they didn't support each other. Maxwell had tried to navigate with Annie through her identity crisis, and he could only conclude that he'd failed. He didn't know if Annie had actually tried to navigate with him through his evolution, but if she had, she'd also failed. This lack of love and support had

had an effect on their son, and that was simply not acceptable.

Maxwell wasn't sure how much Joey understood. The day he moved out, Annie and he sat down with the boy and tried to explain what was going on. They'd consulted books and a child psychologist and presented the situation in age-appropriate terms. Joey spent most of the very brief conversation fidgeting on the couch. He seemed so intent on his SpongeBob action figure that Maxwell couldn't tell how much Joey had absorbed. The next day, Joey spent the night at Maxwell's new place for the first time. He asked some questions about his bed, asked why Maxwell wasn't living at the other house anymore, and then asked whether the TV in the den had the same shows on it that his other TV had. Maxwell knew there would be many additional levels at which Joey would be coming to terms with this change, and he knew he had to be cognizant of his son's reactions to everything, but in the three weeks since, Joey hadn't had a single tantrum or episode of acting out. It was as though he had been carrying the burden of expecting the worst and then, when it happened and the world didn't end, he just recalibrated. Again, Maxwell wasn't kidding himself that there would never be any rough patches, but Joey's returned calm was a good sign.

The past year — and especially the past few months — had certainly jostled Maxwell's notions about his perceptions of the world and his place within it. He'd always seen himself as an everything or nothing kind of guy, the kind of person who shot for the best possible scenario and assumed that falling short meant failure. Now, though, he realized that "everything" came in degrees. His triumvirate of family, love, and career had more nuance than he'd anticipated. He was okay with that.

Maxwell glanced over at the clock on his night table. It was nearly seven-thirty and Joey still wasn't up. He should probably be taking advantage of the opportunity to get a little more sleep himself, but Maxwell had been awakening early every day since the election. Maxwell had had stretches in the past when his mind went into overdrive early in the morning and drove him out of bed. In those other instances, though, his thoughts had centered on problems that needed to be solved. This time, what was pushing him awake was possibility. Possibilities for family. Possibilities for career. Hey, someday, maybe even possibilities for love.

The landing of two feet on the carpet in Joey's room indicated that his son had risen from his long — for him — slumber. Within seconds, Joey was running through the doorway and only a couple of seconds later Joey was bouncing on Maxwell's chest. Joey was definitely getting bigger. If this morning behavior continued until the kid was in kindergarten, Maxwell might need to start wearing catcher's gear to bed.

Joey stopped bouncing and sat on Maxwell's stomach. He slapped both of his small hands on the side of Maxwell's face.

"What are we going to do today?" he said.

"Got me, Pinball. What do you want to do?"

A note from the author

Thank you for reading this novel. This was a challenging story for me to write, because I had to take Maxwell through so much and I knew from the very beginning that there was no way he could come out of this entirely unscathed. I hope you found his journey satisfying and that you feel I treated him okay.

As always, I am very interested in your thoughts, both on this novel and what you'd like to see from the Gold family in the future. If you'd like to write, you can reach me at michael@michaelbaronbooks.com. I'd love to hear from you.

Warmest regards,
Michael